TORI CARRINGTON
Possession

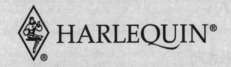

HARLEQUIN®

TORONTO • NEW YORK • LONDON
AMSTERDAM • PARIS • SYDNEY • HAMBURG
STOCKHOLM • ATHENS • TOKYO • MILAN • MADRID
PRAGUE • WARSAW • BUDAPEST • AUCKLAND

Some like it hot! We wholeheartedly dedicate this book to fellow readers who like a little—or a lot!— of spice with their romance novels.

And, as always, to our editor Brenda Chin, who is our third collaborator in all of our Harlequin endeavors. Thank you!

ISBN 0-373-79216-6

POSSESSION

Copyright © 2005 by Lori and Tony Karayianni.

www.eHarlequin.com

Printed in U.S.A.

Praise for Tori Carrington...

"One of the genre's most beloved authors."
—*Rendezvous*

"This author sure knows how to create convincing characters with real-life drama. The highly potent emotionalism of all the characters adds to the powerful chemistry between these two, making for a dynamically charged sensual tale that's good for more than one read."
—*Rendezvous* on *Forbidden*

"A smash hit! Don't miss this one! These characters sizzle and have a chemistry that turns their weaknesses into strengths. A real winner!"
—*Romantic Times* (4$^1/_2$ stars) on *Just Between Us*

"Tori Carrington is an unparalleled storyteller with an imagination that is absolutely matchless. These authors are extraordinary and have a true gift for putting their own special brand on anything they touch."
—*Rendezvous* on *Private Investigations*

"Tori Carrington's latest, *Red-Hot & Reckless,* is an edgy, erotic fantasy nicely balanced by solid conflict and strongly drawn characters."
—*Romantic Times*

"Laced with intense emotion, humor, and some of the sharpest dialogue ever written."
—*Rendezvous* on *The P.I. Who Loved Her*

Blaze™

Dear Reader,

DANGEROUS LIAISONS…the series name alone brings all sorts of decadent images to mind, doesn't it? Now add New Orleans' French Quarter and the sultry Louisiana bayous to the mix and, well, you end up with a recipe base that's guaranteed to be hot, hot, hot.

In *Possession,* sexy Cajun and ex-marine sniper Claude Lafitte appears every bit the gentleman pirate like his rumored ancestor…until beautiful FBI agent Akela Brooks wrongly suspects him of murder, sending him on the run and forcing him to rely on his bayou roots in order to clear his name. The two match wits at every turn. Only, Akela is completely unprepared for the doors of sexual wonders Claude opens up to her. But as the story unfolds, Claude begins to wonder exactly who is possessing whom.

Ooo-wee! This one nearly scorched our fingers just writing it. We'd love to hear what you think. Contact us at P.O. Box 12271, Toledo, OH 43612 (we'll respond with a signed bookplate, newsletter and bookmark), or visit us on the Web at www.toricarrington.com for fun drawings.

Here's wishing you love, romance and *hot* reading.

Lori & Tony Karayianni
aka Tori Carrington

1

HEAVEN TO CLAUDE LAFITTE was a night spent in the arms of a beautiful woman. And, given his past, that was probably as close as he was ever going to get to the pearly gates guarded by St. Pete.

He lay across the old iron bed, the particular beautiful woman he'd met the night before asleep next to him, her curved hip bare, his tanned hand contrasting with her pale flesh in the hazy late-morning light streaming in from the window. When dawn had arrived, he pondered whether to slip from the rented room in New Orleans's French Quarter like a shadow, or wait and bid his partner the adieu she deserved.

He sighed contentedly, taking in her flowing lines, her blond hair, the scent of her, of them, filling the small room. She'd said her name was Claire. No last name. Just as he'd simply been Claude—at least to her. The small hotel's personnel, on the other hand, was very familiar with him, because he came here often, preferring the simplicity of the hotel over his own apartment if only because a hotel room seemed to suit the temporary nature of his occasional liaisons.

Women. Once, a long time ago, he'd taken great relish in counting how many he'd seduced into his bed. Now he merely enjoyed their company, the pleasure he found in them as varied as the women themselves. It didn't matter where they came from, if they were natives or from foreign countries, each of them provided an enticing escape.

Escape?

Claude removed his hand from Claire's warm skin and rubbed his face. There was nothing from which he needed to escape. Life was good. No, life was great. A little more red tape and he would own Lafitte's Louisiana Boats and Tours outright. And while money would be tight for a while, his current circumstances were far removed from the humble upbringing in which he and his brother, Thierry, had been raised. While life in the bayous held a certain wild appeal, your surroundings didn't much matter if your belly was empty and your opportunities scant.

The woman next to him sighed in her sleep and rolled toward him, her breasts pressing against his side. Claude pushed strands of her white blond hair from her face and watched as she smiled and sighed again.

He glanced at his watch. It was Sunday. He didn't have to be anywhere. Maybe he'd pay for the room for a few extra hours and treat her to breakfast. Beignets and café au lait.

Then maybe afterward they could pick up where they'd left off....

AKELA BROOKS'S plain navy-blue suit was too heavy for this October morning in the Quarter. Now that she'd relocated to the New Orleans FBI field office, she'd have to do some shopping for suits of lightweight material: breathable linens, more generous cut cotton blends, skirts, rather than the slacks she preferred.

While the thought of shopping might brighten others' day, it made Akela frown. Something she'd been doing a lot since Friday when she'd been given her first assignment at the field office. Correction. She hadn't so much been given an assignment as she'd been buried with follow-up work on cases that were otherwise closed.

It didn't help knowing that she'd expected it. She hadn't requested to be reassigned to the New Orleans office because of advancement opportunities, but because she'd wanted...no, needed, to be closer to her family. It was time—long past time if she was truthful. But she wasn't much into delving into the past. Now was now and if you spent all your time looking backward, you might trip over a stone in front of you. And then where would you be aside from facedown on the asphalt?

Her low heels clicked against the sidewalk, the sights and smells on Bourbon Street abundant, but the people noticeably scarce this early on a Sunday morning. Early? It was past eleven. But here eleven was early. The cry of a trumpet came from a jazz bar a couple of doors up. Someone swept debris from the curb. A car—allowed to pass at this time of day, but barred access later on when the street teemed with tourists—cruised by filled with a family probably headed to church.

Akela shrugged out of her jacket, folded it over her arm, then straightened her white, sleeveless blouse. While New Orleans was her home, this New Orleans—the Quarter, jazz, drink and decadence—wasn't. The Brookses lived uptown in the Garden District and pretty much stayed there, venturing out only to attend charity balls in swanky hotels and to go to the opera and the museum and various art gallery happenings.

Oh, she'd come to the Quarter a few times. Everyone in New Orleans eventually did at one time or another. One occasion, in particular, stuck out in her mind. She'd been sixteen and Mardi Gras had been in full swing. She'd gotten sick from too much liquor and had woken up on the front porch of her parents' estate, her neck draped in beads, and under her shirt someone had drawn red smiley faces around her breasts with lipstick that had been hell to get off.

It hadn't been so much what had happened that rowdy night that had scared her off returning to the Quarter. Rather it had been that she couldn't *remember* what had transpired. Not being in control of her actions frightened her in a way few things could.

Of course, it helped that she'd never been much for rebellion. No, she'd saved that for one single whopper when she was twenty and going to Tulane University: Namely she'd broken from tradition and sought a career in law enforcement.

Her society-conscious mother had yet to forgive her for that transgression. Strangely, in Patsy Brooks's eyes the move even overshadowed Akela's marriage and divorce to a fellow agent that had resulted in her now four-year-old daughter, Daisy. Patsy was of the school convinced that impulsive acts, like the one that had inspired Akela to apply to the FBI, were not allowed. A lady of a certain standing did not go around brandishing a gun. She should achieve a well-rounded education and work in the legal or medical field until she married and bore children, and then her family would become her priority, along with certain charitable endeavors.

Her mother's staunch and unforgiving beliefs were what made Akela seek posts as far away from New Orleans as possible—Quantico, then Boston.

Now it was her daughter's need to be surrounded by family that loved her that had brought Akela back home. And if Akela longed for the same, well, she wasn't ready to consider that right now.

Her heel caught between bricks and she stumbled.

"Careful, *cher*," a man said as he caught her, keeping her from twisting her ankle.

Her gaze shifted from the large, dark hand on her arm to the warm green eyes of the man it belonged to. A Cajun. Had to be. A big, hulking, stunning example of a Cajun.

She took in his suggestive grin and the confident way he stood, as if there was no doubt his chivalry would be well received. And, Akela realized with a shock of awareness, it was. Something swept from him to her and back again, a current of something fundamental, primal, that brought heat to her cheeks and made her blood thicken.

"Thanks," she said almost breathlessly.

He murmured something that was probably the equivalent of "you're welcome" and continued moving past her in the opposite direction, breaking the connection.

Akela watched him go, drinking in the casually snug black T-shirt and the bunched muscles underneath, the athletic tightness of his rear end, the tousled look of his dark blond hair, as if he'd just rolled out of bed. She filled her lungs with the heavy air, noticing the tingle of restlessness zinging along her nerve endings. It was all too easy to imagine herself stretched across crisp white sheets, a man like him nudging her bare thighs apart with his knee. At the thought, she became aware of the heavy New Orleans air dampening her skin and the delicate wings of butterflies teasing the inside of her stomach, making her feel weightless and light.

She swallowed hard, her throat tight, her heart beating a little bit faster.

Turning she headed toward Hotel Josephine, a small structure, likely an ex-bordello, on the edge of the Quarter.

Yes, there were going to be a lot of adjustments she'd have to make. New Orleans was worlds away from Quantico, and Boston, where she'd been assigned for the past six years. Here, time moved at a slower pace, probably more because of the thick humidity that was always present in the air than due to any conscious decision. There was a pervasive haze that seemed to mute human morality, making lazy decadence not only acceptable but the norm.

In Virginia and New England, women expected to be wined and dined. And sex…well, sex was never a foregone conclusion. Here in New Orleans it was understood that when a man of the type she'd passed in the street asked you for a date, he was asking if you were interested in sex. If food or other entertainment was a part of the package, well, that was an extra.

Here in the Quarter, sex—more specifically hot, sweaty, multiple-orgasm sex—was its own reward.

And for the first time in a very long time, she found the idea of allowing more primitive instincts to control her and her body appealing. More than appealing, she felt as if she pulsed with the need to feel a man's hands on her, stroking her, coaxing to the surface emotions and needs she had long buried.

Akela stood outside the high, narrow double blue doors to Hotel Josephine, pondering how, when set against the backdrop of the Quarter, her life in New England emerged dull and colorless.

A couple walked leisurely through the doors to the hotel, the woman wearing a slinky slip dress and clinging to her partner in an undeniably sexual way. Akela couldn't help but watch them, both fascinated and curious about them and the uninhibited lives they lived.

She shrugged back into her jacket as she walked through the airy hotel lobby, noticing the green courtyard beyond, thinking the place needed a good paint job and thorough cleaning. Then again, she didn't think the clientele came here for the atmosphere. Or maybe they did. The place seemed to reek of forbidden affairs and passionate trysts.

She flashed her ID at the pretty woman sitting fanning herself on the other side of the check-in counter, the whirring ceiling fan doing little to ease the heat.

"Agent Brooks, FBI," Akela said, clapping the ID closed then slipping it back into the pocket of her jacket. "I'm here to talk to Pierre Deville."

The provocative, slightly dark-skinned woman regarded her through half-lidded eyes as if visits from FBI agents were the rule rather than the exception. "Room 2B."

"Thank you."

Akela began climbing the curving staircase edged with wrought-iron railings. A shrill scream stopped her cold. A woman's scream of fear.

Akela took the steps two at a time, reaching for the firearm that was strapped into a holder inside her jacket. She emerged onto the second floor, gun in hand, safety off, spotting a young woman in a maid's uniform holding fresh linens. She was standing outside an open door, staring inside.

"FBI," Akela said. "Move to the side."

The maid didn't appear to hear her so Akela physically shifted her away then positioned herself where the maid had been standing. Inside the room a woman was sprawled across the mattress of a double bed, her eyes staring unseeingly at the ceiling, her throat cut.

CAFÉ AU LAIT AND BEIGNETS. Breakfast of champions. Walking up Bourbon Street, Claude carried a bag with two covered cups and another with the sugar-sprinkled French doughnuts. The neighborhood was just beginning to stir to life. Where earlier, musicians had tuned their instruments, now full bands played, trying to entice tourists and locals alike into the air-conditioned depths of their places of business.

"*Bonjour,* Claude."

He glanced over at the scantily clad woman standing in the doorway of a popular strip club and grinned, giving her a half salute with a finger to his eyebrow. "Morning, Janette. You're looking particularly beautiful today."

His mother, Olivie Lafitte, bless her heart, had taught both her boys that while compliments cost them little to give, they could be priceless to the person receiving them. Paying Janette one came as easily to Claude as his leisurely stride.

Her smile widened. "Let's hope that means some good tips."

He chuckled. "I'm sure it will, *ma chérie*. I'm sure it will."

He was familiar with Chantal and her girls, sometimes bringing visiting associates by to help contribute to the private school tuition of Janette's daughter, and the college fund of the younger prostitute.

The sound of a siren turned his head in the other direction and he stepped back up onto the banquette, watching as an NOPD patrol car sped by, lights blazing, then skidded to a stop outside Josephine's.

Claude slowed his steps. Another thing his mother had always taught him and his brother was always to be leery of the law.

He wasn't entirely sure of the motivation behind that advice. Perhaps it was Cajun custom that justice be doled out by their peers. Or maybe the belief went even further back, to Jean Lafitte, who was rumored to be his great-great grandfather. Of course, every Lafitte claimed the same connection to the notorious gentleman pirate.

A part of his wariness toward officers of the law also stemmed from the trouble he'd gotten into when he'd left the bayou at fourteen and survived on the streets of New Orleans for the next several years any way he could, which had included illegal activity. He'd used his knowledge of the bayous, combined it with the criminal education he'd received on the streets, and at nineteen had ended up being stabbed in the back, both literally and figuratively, left to bleed to death in a dark alley after a deal gone bad. A judge had given him a choice: five years in prison or a stint in the military.

He'd chosen the military.

Those days were behind him now, but never far—which was what prompted him to go around to the rear entrance to Josephine's. He climbed the back stairs to the room he'd rented until later that afternoon. He stopped when he reached the hall, finding the door open and the woman he'd bumped into on the street earlier tucking a gun into her jacket.

Claire…

The stranger in the door turned and their eyes met. As on the street, he was caught off guard by the dark grayness of her eyes, the fullness of her mouth, her innate sexuality in stark contrast to the severe cut of her suit and her stiff demeanor.

He was aware she was moving, reaching back inside her jacket. He watched as she hauled out her firearm and pointed it in his direction, both hands braced against the weapon.

"FBI. Stay where you are."

Call him paranoid, but Claude Lafitte of Barataria Bayou in Jefferson Parish had no intention of doing anything of the kind.

2

WHAT HAD BEGUN as a run-of-the-mill follow-up had turned into something much more dark and dangerous.

Akela held her hands steady as she pointed her standard FBI issue 10mm semiautomatic weapon at the man who had just come up the back stairs holding two plain white bags.

The man who had steadied her on the street.

The realization hit her at the same time she suspected he was going to make a run for it.

She was a crack shot. It was one of the talents that had propelled her to the top of her class at the Academy. Imagine, a good girl from a high-society family being able to shoot the tail feather off a mallard at a hundred yards and leave the duck none the wiser.

At this short distance, she could render the man immobile with a simple squeeze of the trigger.

But while shooting to disable a suspect was acceptable by FBI standards—the Bureau's leeway having increased in that regard with the looming terrorist threat—she didn't think the NOPD would appreciate her putting a piece of lead into their suspect. Because even though she was there by sheer luck, and she was a federal law-enforcement officer, the local police department would have jurisdiction over the homicide case and over the suspect she was staring at down the barrel of her gun.

And that he was the suspect in question, the Claude Lafitte the woman at the front desk had told her had rented the room for a few more hours, wasn't in doubt if only because the other three rooms on the floor had already been vacated and stood empty.

She heard footsteps on the second set of stairs behind her. She glanced to find two uniformed NOPD officers, guns drawn, running into the hall. When she looked back toward the suspect, she found him gone, the bags he'd been holding on the top step.

"Damn!"

Dropping her gun to her side, she dashed for the other set of stairs, watching as the man disappeared down them. She ran after him, yelling for him to freeze. She hit the back courtyard at a dead run, edging around tables and small trees then bursting into the lobby through open double French doors. One of the police officers came back down the front stairs and reached the open area at the same time she did. She shook her head to indicate she didn't know where the suspect was.

An arm snaked around her from behind and hauled her against a rock-hard chest.

"We meet again, *cher*," the suspect whispered into her ear, yanking her closer and prying the gun she held from her frozen fingers.

Never in her six years as an agent had she lost control of her weapon.

Earlier, sexual awareness had made Akela's heart beat fast; now pure adrenaline had it slamming against her chest. She moved to jam her heel against his instep. He easily avoided the attempt along with the elbow she simultaneously tried to land to his midsection, the double move a standard one designed to catch the assailant off guard so she could gain the upper hand.

He easily prevented her from twisting from his grasp, his strength more than she could challenge without the benefit of the other two moves.

He cocked her gun and pressed the cold muzzle against her temple.

"My worst fear is being killed with my own firearm."

The words her Quantico weapons instructor had said on the first day of class rang through her mind. She hadn't understood the significance of the fear until this minute.

Lafitte tsked the NOPD officer and his partner who joined him. "No, no, no. You won't want to be doing that, friend."

Akela realized he was nudging her closer to the front door.

"Hostage situations never end well for the hostage taker," she told her captor, her voice laced with steel as she dug her fingernails into the arm holding her.

She felt his warm breath on her ear. "I imagine they don't usually turn out well for the hostage, either, so I'd suggest you behave.

"Back," Lafitte ordered the officers.

Akela thought of the difference in shooting procedures and wished two fellow FBI agents were with her rather than NOPD officers. An agent would have shot Lafitte already, no matter the danger to her.

"Back, I say." The gun disappeared from her temple as Lafitte waved it at the two policemen.

"Claude," the woman manning the front desk said, her head appearing from behind the counter. "Don't do this."

"Shush, Josie," he told her.

Akela took full advantage of his distraction and tore out of his hold at the same time as she reached for his outstretched arm holding the gun. He easily grabbed her right hand and twisted it, forcing her to her knees in a crude but effective move that left her feeling as if he'd cracked a bone with his strong grip.

"Put your guns down. Now!" Lafitte ordered. "Josie, go collect them."

"I'll do no such thing."

Lafitte aimed the gun he held at the counter and squeezed off a shot. The loud sound reverberated against the high ceiling as a bullet splintered molding off the side of the check-in counter.

Josie scurried to do as he asked.

Lafitte dragged Akela back to her feet and held her face-to-face with him. Up this close, she could see the blue flecks in his green eyes, feel the heat of his body permeate the front of her blouse, feel the tips of her breasts chafe against his chest as she struggled against him.

"You're coming with me," he said. "It would be best if you didn't fight me."

"Best for whom?"

He grinned at her.

Akela's breath caught in her throat.

Then just like that, Lafitte was pushing her through the front doors and with a knowledge of the Quarter that far surpassed Akela's, he snaked a path through clubs and bars and strip joints until Akela wasn't sure she'd be able to find her way back without a map.

Within minutes they stood behind a large Buick. He tightened the arm around her neck and she gasped for air, fighting him as he unlocked the trunk then moved so he could jerk her hands behind her back. Akela kicked backward, catching him in the knee with her heel, then shot forward, out of his grasp and toward safety. She got three feet when he grasped her and yanked her back.

Akela sucked in a breath.

"My intention is not to hurt you," he said, twining strong fingers into her hair as he worked with his other hand to wind what felt like duct tape around one of her wrists.

"Well, then, you failed."

"Not my fault."

"What would you have me do as an agent of the FBI?" she asked. "Go willingly?"

"It would make things easier." Something in his voice made her pretty sure he was grinning again.

He released her hair and grabbed her free arm,

winding duct tape around that one, as well, then binding her wrists together behind her back.

Akela tried to jerk away from him. "You're free. You don't need me anymore."

He had finished tying her hands yet stood still behind her. "Mmm. Maybe what you say is true."

She whipped around to face him, damp tendrils of her hair sticking to her cheek. "So release me."

"Then again, maybe keeping you is my ticket out of the city." Maintaining a restraining arm against her legs to keep her from kneeing him, he wound more duct tape around her ankles, then opened the car trunk and, more gently than she would have thought possible, placed her inside.

He moved to close the hood. "Claire…is she…"

Akela squinted at him. The name of the victim at the hotel had been Claire Laraway.

Surely he wasn't asking her if she was dead? He was the one who had killed her.

"Just so you know," she said. "Very soon that gun's going to be back in my hands. And when it is, this conversation is going to go very differently."

He unrolled some more tape then bit off a short length of it with white, even teeth.

"I already think there's been enough conversation," he said, then put the tape over her mouth and closed the trunk.

CLAUDE DROVE through the narrow city streets, his stomach tight, his senses on high alert. The car was clean and couldn't immediately be traced back to him because it was registered to his and his brother's company, not to him personally.

He braked at a stop sign and watched as a squad car cruised by on the street in front of him. Clean or not, it wouldn't keep his likeness from showing up on the computer screens on every squad car in town. He reached for an LSU ball cap on the floor of the backseat then smoothed his longish hair back and put the cap on. After switching on the radio that was set to a zydeco station, he cranked up the volume, both to drown out the sound of the pretty agent kicking against the trunk and to make it appear to those he passed that he had nothing more pressing on his mind than making a run for a gallon of milk.

Claire was dead. He didn't have to be a genius to figure that out. When he'd left her, she'd been smiling, half-asleep, hugging a pillow between her bare breasts, her skin rosy pink, her eyes full of naughty suggestion. Acid lined his stomach at the thought of all that life being drained from her, and mere minutes after he'd crawled out of a bed they'd shared for the night—a bed he'd had every intention of returning to.

Instead, he'd returned to find another beautiful

woman holding a gun on him and to learn that Claire was dead.

His hands tightened on the steering wheel, tension radiating from his every muscle.

"One of these days your wicked ways are going to catch up with you, Jean-Claude."

The warning had come from Thierry's mouth two years ago, just after his brother had married Brigitte, and Claude had taken his fill of the maid of honor's generous attentions.

"One morning you're going to wake up to find a gun pressed to your forehead by a jealous husband or a jilted lover. Then where will you be?"

He'd chuckled at his brother, who hadn't been all that unlike him—at least until he'd met Brigitte.

Claude ran a hand over his face. Somehow he didn't think Thier would have predicted things would go down quite this way when he'd forecasted Claude's doom.

Some minutes later, as he entered the on-ramp for Highway 10, he realized that without really knowing where he was going, his instincts had sent him in the direction of the bayous, where a man could disappear as easily as a gator in the deep swamps and towering cypresses.

Another kick to the trunk.

Claude turned up the music louder and let the car lead him home and to safety.

As for the woman…he'd decide what to do with her when the time came.

3

AKELA'S LEGS threatened to cramp up. She struggled against the restraints at her ankles and her wrists, then gave another angry kick at the backseat of the high-end vehicle, glad only that the trunk was large and she at least had a little room to maneuver.

The best she could figure was that she'd been in the car for at least half an hour, although she couldn't be sure because she knew that in such situations the passage of time became distorted, so that five minutes seemed like an hour, essentially proving Einstein's theory of relativity. Around ten minutes into the drive, she'd heard the unmistakable sound of the tires hitting a stretch of elevated pavement, possibly over a bridge. Canal Street? The causeway? The T Bridge? She couldn't be sure.

She felt around for the cell phone she managed to shift from her jacket pocket, although she couldn't read the display. She'd blindly pushed the 911 button, but with her mouth covered, she couldn't tell the answering officer where she was. And since caller ID didn't extend to cell phones yet, it was pretty much a lost cause.

The car began to slow. Staring up at the dark roof of the trunk, Akela closed her cell phone and fumbled to put it safely back into her right jacket pocket. The small piece of modern technology could be all that stood between her and freedom. And she couldn't chance that Lafitte would take it away from her when he finally reached his destination.

Thankfully about fifteen minutes ago he had turned down the volume of the radio so the speakers so near her ear no longer pulsed with the sounds of washboard-heavy zydeco. Still, Akela didn't think her hearing would ever be the same. She knew why he'd done it, of course: to mask her attempts to make as much noise as she could by thrashing against the trunk.

The car shuddered, likely having hit a pothole. She squinted into the darkness, listening hard, and heard the unmistakable sound of gravel hitting the undercarriage. They must have moved from a paved road to a cruder means of passage. The car dipped again, and she bounced, her hip coming down hard on what she figured was the nut holding the spare tire in place under the thin carpeting.

Where was he taking her?

The sound of gravel was replaced by what she thought might be dirt.

Fear wadded in her throat. If Claude Lafitte had killed Claire Laraway, what did he have in mind for her?

Louisiana was not without its serial killers. Russell Ellwood was arrested in 1998, suspected of killing twenty-six people in an eight-year period. Then there was the more recent Bayou Killer, who was believed to have killed at least seven young women.

Finally, the car stopped. The absence of movement caused Akela to slump in relief against the bottom of the trunk. The reaction was short-lived as she heard the clinking of keys and then was blinded by the sudden burst of light when the trunk lid sprang up.

"Hope you weren't too uncomfortable."

She struggled to sit up. She felt hands on her shoulders and Lafitte lifted her out of the trunk just as easily as he had put her inside. With her legs still bound, his restraining arm was all that prevented her from falling to the hard ground face-first.

And it was, indeed, ground beneath her feet. More specifically, dirt. Avoiding looking at her captor, she glanced around at the towering cypresses and live oaks covered in Spanish moss, the kudzu and the swamp that surrounded them. Cicadas buzzed loudly and somewhere something dropped into the water, causing a rippling plop. She had little doubt that Lafitte had taken her to one of the bayous surrounding New Orleans. But which one? Was the Mississippi River or the Gulf of Mexico closer? Did people heavily inhabit the area, or were gators the main occupants?

"Where are we?" she asked as he closed the trunk.

Of course, her question was little more than a hum because she still had the tape over her mouth.

Finally, she looked into Lafitte's face. He squinted at her, as if trying to read her intentions, then sighed and scooped her up like a sack of flour.

"There will be time enough for conversation later."

Akela couldn't help her expression of shock, even though she'd been trained to keep careful control over her reactions.

Later? In most hostage situations, the hostage was released the moment he or she was no longer needed. So why was Claude Lafitte keeping her? And what did he plan to do with her once he was done?

For a man so big, he was surprisingly gentle. Though the earth beneath his booted feet was harsh and uneven, he held her in such a way that prevented any jarring. Akela stared at his strong pro-

file. Tousled dark blond hair spiked over his broad
forehead. His features were too craggy to be considered handsome, but somehow when combined
with his full mouth and intense green eyes, he
commanded attention. She caught a partial
glimpse of a tattoo on his left arm. It looked like
a crude, green snake slithering out from under the
sleeve of his T-shirt.

His gaze met hers and he gave her a crooked
grin. "Almost there."

Almost where? she wanted to ask, but couldn't.

She looked around again at the backdrop of the
bayou. As a native of New Orleans, she was familiar with the Crescent City's surrounding swamps,
but much like the city's French Quarter, she'd
never spent an extended amount of time there. She
preferred air-conditioned surroundings as opposed
to the wet, oppressive heat she felt pressing in on
her from all sides here. It was almost as if the
swamp itself hung in the air.

She heard his boots hit something other than dirt
and realized he was climbing a set of wood stairs.

The small house could have been any one of a
thousand just like it: one story, elevated on stilts
to prevent the wetlands from claiming it, with
wood shingles in need of a fresh coat of varnish.
A cry from a bird drew her attention upward and

she stared at a vulture perched watching, as if hoping the trussed-up package Lafitte carried would eventually be presented to him.

Akela's feet met with the solid wooden platform of the porch. She blinked at Lafitte as he pulled a knife out of his pocket. With a clean whoosh of metal against metal, the four-inch blade popped up, closer than was comfortable. He bent over and cut the tape at her ankles.

Akela fought not to show her relief.

Lafitte watched her closely. "What, you thought I had other intentions?"

She opened her mouth to speak. A lesson in futility as the duct tape prevented her from enunciating clearly.

Lafitte leaned closer to her, considered the tape, then looked into her eyes. Akela's breath caught as she read the unmistakable suggestiveness in his eyes.

"No one's going to hear you out here, *ma catin*," he murmured.

Akela froze as his nose rubbed briefly against hers, nothing more than a feather's touch. Her reaction was anything but brief or feathery. Fire seemed to burn through her veins at the purposely sexual move.

"Just the same," he said, "you make any noises

that don't have to do with conversation…or plea-sure, and the tape goes back on."

Pleasure?

She nearly choked as he slowly pulled the tape from her sensitive skin, her breasts feeling sud-denly tender, her body going on alert.

"That's good," he said, apparently approving of the fact that she hadn't screamed.

She turned around. "My hands?"

He squinted at her through the sun that dappled through the canopy of live oaks. "Stay the way they are for now."

Part of her FBI training had been learning how to maneuver efficiently with her hands tied behind her back. If the bindings were low enough on her wrists, she could even contort herself so that her hands were in front rather than behind her. But the thick tape allowed for no such movement. And the surrounding remote terrain guaranteed that even if she did make a run for it, she wouldn't get far.

He turned her back around to face him, his gaze holding hers captive as he placed his hands on her shoulders. Akela swore she could feel his heat even though the temperature had to be somewhere in the nineties and the cloth of her jacket separated them. He slid his fingers up to her neck, placing his thumbs near her pulse points. She swallowed thickly, reading almost a smile and something darker in his eyes. Then he moved his hands down her arms, causing her to shiver in instant response.

She gasped when he moved his hands from the sleeves of her jacket to inside the front flaps.

"Hold still," he said quietly.

Akela didn't think it was possible to hold still. Not with him touching her so intimately. And while it should be her instinct to survive which prompted her heart to beat fast, she suspected it was her growing awareness of him as a man that made her pulse race and restlessness settle into the core of her limbs.

He pulled her ID wallet from her inside breast pocket, his actions breaking Akela from whatever Cajun spell he'd momentarily put her under. Next he took her cell phone from her right front pocket.

He opened her ID and seemed to compare her with her picture.

"Brooks, Akela, you'll excuse me if I say you're much more beautiful in person."

She turned her head away, feeling naked without the accoutrements of her job. During her ride in the trunk, some of her hair had escaped her tight French twist, and tendrils now stuck to her damp face.

He pulled her gun from his waistband and put it and the cell phone inside a large and apparently empty water barrel, then secured the top. After he pocketed her ID, he pulled a wood-slatted chair on the porch closer to her. "Sit. The place will be hot as hot gets until it airs out a bit."

Akela remained standing, watching as he retrieved a key from inside a coffee can in the middle of dozens of others on the corner of the porch then opened the front door of the house. After sparing her a glance, he went inside.

And Akela immediately turned toward the staircase.

Before she got two steps, Lafitte was tugging her back and forcing her to sit on the chair backward, so that her front was against the back and her legs over the sides, making her skirt ride up.

"Ah, even a man such as myself can't help but take such bad manners personally."

Akela raised her brows high. "How do you expect me to take your kidnapping of me?"

His small smile proved he wasn't beneath appreciating irony. "Fair enough." He slowly waggled a finger at her, then tapped the tip of her nose, his gaze seeming to linger a little longer than necessary on her lips, which felt swollen from the tape. "But try that again and I'll be forced to take greater measures to ensure such attempts aren't an option."

He turned toward the door again, disappearing inside the one-story house. She heard windows being opened, fans being switched on. She took advantage of the temporary freedom to look around. The bayous stretched out in front of the house with nothing breaking the green, mossy landscape. Not a house or boat to be seen. She couldn't make out the sound of any cars, meaning they were far enough away from any major roads not to be heard.

The hinges on the screen door squeaked and she snapped her head to find Lafitte stepping back outside. He'd taken off his T-shirt and was wiping the sweat from his face with it. Akela couldn't help taking in the rock-hard ridges of his abs. The thickness of his biceps. The smoothness of his tanned skin. A jagged scar ran under his right nipple—an old wound that by the looks of it had never been tended properly. He turned from her and lifted the lid off another barrel, submerging his shirt into the water inside, giving her full view of another scar on the long flanks of his lower back near the waist of his jeans—jeans that hugged his bottom and thighs to pure male perfection.

She caught sight of the rest of the tattoo she'd seen earlier on his upper left bicep. It had indeed been a snake. It formed the *S* in USMC. United

States Marine Corps. The snake possibly signifying he had been a sniper, which would explain why he was comfortable around guns, and also why he seemed to know his way around a volatile situation.

She turned her face away from him.

Who was this man? And why was she attracted to him as much as she was repulsed by him?

There was nothing but the sound of a kingfisher calling overhead as Lafitte filled his shirt with water then squeezed it over his head, dampening his hair until it shone darkly, droplets clinging to his skin.

"Did she suffer?"

Akela wasn't sure she'd heard the question at first. Lafitte still had his back to her and was now dousing his face with the water.

He glanced at her over a broad shoulder, his hair dripping down into his face, making him look even more like a wild predator.

She cleared her throat. "I don't know," she said. "Did she?"

He went still for a couple of long moments, and then he turned, T-shirt in hand. "Claire was still very much alive when I left her." A shadowy look that could have been pain shifted over his face. Then he wrung out the shirt and hung it over the railing. "And happy."

He caught her looking at his abs and she quickly looked away.

Even given her current circumstances, Akela couldn't help but appreciate the fine image he made. Men like Claude Lafitte graced the covers of half the books at the bookstore. All Louisiana would have to do in order to improve tourism was to issue a poster of him looking exactly the way he did now, the untamed bayou surrounding him, and women would come in swarms.

Yes, she admitted, even she was having a hard time ignoring the sexual aura he exuded in waves. She'd felt it when she'd run into him on Bourbon Street, before she'd gone inside the hotel to find the woman dead: a sort of fundamental electrical current, an awareness that drew a healthy female to a virile male.

"What was your relationship to the deceased?" she asked quietly, making the mistake of looking up into his face for his reaction—a mistake because his reaction was a dark and dangerously sexy look.

"I should think that's obvious."

"The only thing that's obvious is the possibility that you are her killer."

"I don't make a habit out of killing women I enjoy," he said quietly. Too quietly. "But I suppose I should be relieved that you admit there's a possibility that I didn't kill her."

She shifted in the chair. "You didn't answer my question."

"No, I didn't." He fell silent for long moments and she thought he might ignore her question altogether. Then he looked at her, his face devoid of expression. "My mother, bless her soul, taught me the art of discretion."

Akela refused to give up. "Long-term or short-term?"

"Miss Claire and I became acquainted last night."

Acquainted. Now there was a new word for it.

It had been obvious by the dead woman's state of undress, and the appearance of the bed she'd been lying in, that she and Claude Lafitte had become very well acquainted indeed.

He crossed over to stand in front of her, putting his bare torso mere inches away from her face. Akela suddenly had a difficult time breathing.

"It's not what you think, between me and Claire," he said.

She watched as he ran his hand through his hair.

"Then again, maybe it is. I don't know. All I know is that I didn't bring her any harm."

This time, Akela looked away from the conviction on his handsome face.

"You must be hot," he said, helping her to her feet. "Let's get you out of those clothes."

4

AKELA BROOKS WAS WOUND UP tighter than a fishing line. Of course, that might have something to do with the fact that her presence wasn't exactly voluntary. But he'd never had a woman look at him in fear. And he hated that he'd ignited that in her.

"I'm not going to ravish you, Agent Brooks. Just trying to help you cool off, that's all," he muttered, turning her around so that her bottom was facing him. And despite circumstances, he couldn't help noticing what a fine bottom it was, too. As he cut the tape from her wrists and slid her suit jacket down her arms, he saw that Akela was finely shaped. He supposed her career demanded she be in prime physical condition. But he suspected that she didn't realize how perfectly made her body was for the joys of sexual pleasure.

Then again hadn't sexual pleasure landed him in the middle of this mess?

He methodically stripped her blouse off then

unbuttoned the back of her skirt, allowing it to drop to her feet, leaving her in a simple white slip that looked not at all simple on the stunningly attractive woman.

Claude caught himself running the backs of his knuckles along the exposed nape of her neck and upper back. Goose bumps ran up her bare arms as she shivered.

When he realized what he was doing, he stopped.

"Come on," he said, grasping the back of her arm and urging her toward the door to the house.

He had to give her credit for not saying anything as he moved her toward the double bed in the corner of the one-room house. But her response to his actions was evidenced in the puckering of her nipples beneath her thin slip and bra and the thick way she swallowed. He supposed it wasn't every day that a woman used to being in control had that same control stripped away from her.

He motioned for her to sit on the bed and when she did, after a moment's hesitation, he noticed the way she kept her thighs tightly pulled together and her back reed straight.

Claude clamped a handcuff attached to the wrought-iron headboard to her right wrist.

This did get a reaction as she snapped her face

up to stare at him. "Why am I not surprised you have cuffs already waiting?"

"And who's to say I didn't attach them when I opened the house?"

Her gaze skittered away and slight color spilled across her cheeks.

Claude caught her chin in his hand, wondering at the contrast of his thick, calloused skin against her flawless, smooth face.

"I didn't bring you here to seduce you, *cher*," he said quietly.

"Then why did you bring me here?"

"To give me time to figure everything out."

He forced himself to turn away from the curiously probing look in her eyes and grabbed a towel. "I'll be only a shout away."

"I have to go to the bathroom."

He stopped, but didn't turn to face her. "Let me guess. It hit you at the same time the handcuffs did."

"Are you going to let me go or not?"

"Not," he said after a long moment, then slung the towel over his shoulder. "I won't be long."

"Is that a promise or a threat?"

"I suppose that depends on your point of view."

He turned and headed for the door, listening to the squeak of the box springs as she shifted on the bed. He heard her cuss viciously under her breath as she apparently realized there was no quick way out of her restraints.

AKELA YANKED on the cuffs again then felt defeat settle into her muscles. The handcuffs appeared to be police-grade quality and were firmly secured to an iron headboard that was bolted to the wall.

Bolted to the wall. The only other place she'd seen beds set up like this was motels and hotels, so that the headboards wouldn't bang against the wall during wild sex.

She closed her eyes and stretched the tension from her neck. Funny how the word *sex* kept popping up every five minutes since she'd been in Claude Lafitte's company. And not because of his sexual connection to a murder victim, either.

It was upsetting to find herself physically attracted to a man who was not only a fugitive from justice but her kidnapper. Oddly, she wasn't in fear for her life, which she figured was the way she should be feeling now, considering the crime he was suspected of. But something on a gut level told her she had nothing to fear from Claude. Nothing, that is, that had anything to do with his harming her.

Of course, the fact that she hadn't been with a man in a long, long time might be partially to blame for her primal awareness of the sexy Cajun. But, still, it didn't come close to explaining everything.

She looked around the simple house that was little more than a functional shack. There was a galley kitchen in the opposite corner. A dresser was in the corner beside the bed. A small dining table and chairs sat next to that. And on her other side was a small living-room arrangement.

She heard running water and turned toward the sound through the nearby open window. There in the backyard Lafitte was stepping under the spray of an outdoor showerhead, a wooden wall exposing his powerful calves and feet at the bottom, and his broad chest and shoulders at the top.

Akela couldn't seem to pry her gaze from him, watching as he lathered up, suds running down his wet skin, sunlight glinting off his soaked hair.

Dear Lord.

She frantically looked around for something with which to pick the lock on the cuffs. The place obviously belonged to a man, so there were no bobby pins lying around. No sunglasses so she could use the earpiece. She reached up with her free hand to check her earrings, but she wore her standard simple studs that weren't long enough to do anything with.

She drew in a deep breath. *Think, goddamn it, think.*

No phone that she could see. Not that that was surprising. No television. No microwave. In fact, aside from a transistor radio on the kitchen counter, and the whirling ceiling fans, there didn't appear to be anything of an electronic nature at all. Even the refrigerator appeared to be gas generated. That didn't bode well because of the possibility that no city electricity at all ran to the house—the fans could easily run from a powerful battery or small generator—which meant that they were more isolated than she feared.

The screen door squeaked and she looked up to find Lafitte wearing his jeans and running the towel along his neck and shoulders. Her body temperature shot up another notch, causing the sweat that had accumulated between her breasts to trickle down to her stomach. Suddenly she was all too aware of her state of undress. And, apparently, so was Lafitte.

He looked at her and she felt his gaze straight down to her core. For a moment she thought he might act on the attraction she saw in his eyes.

Then he switched on the transistor radio on the kitchen counter, picked up a few items and went back outside to the porch, the screen door slapping shut behind him.

Akela virtually melted to the mattress, both disturbed by her attraction to this man, her captor, and frustrated that despite all her training and experience she was essentially chained to his bed.

THE STRAINS OF ZYDECO wafted out on the thick air as Claude walked to the edge of the porch and dialed his brother's business number from his cell phone. The receptionist immediately put him through.

"Jesus, Jean-Claude, what kind of trouble have you gone and gotten yourself mixed up in now?" Thierry said in lieu of hello.

He moved the towel on his shoulder to the railing alongside his wet T-shirt. He'd hoped the police hadn't gotten to his brother yet, that they had slowed their determination to track him down. Obviously the hope had been in vain.

He looked through the screen and watched Akela try to crane her neck so she might hear his end of the conversation.

"Have you really kidnapped an FBI agent?" his brother asked.

"Aye, that I have."

"Mon dieu."

The fact that his brother was treating him as if it was only yesterday when he'd last been in trouble, instead of over a decade ago, added to his disquiet.

"Look, Their, I didn't call to get the third degree from you. I need the number of a good attorney."

"Did you do it?"

"Murder that woman?" He ran his hand over his face. "Do you even have to ask?"

Silence for long moments, then a sigh. "No."

"Good then. Find that number for me, won't you, brother? I'll call back in ten minutes."

He rang off then ran his thumb over the lighted numbers of the display. He wasn't sure how sophisticated surveillance techniques were, but he wasn't about to chance being traced through some sort of satellite GPS system. So he determined to keep any calls he made brief and to the point, and his phone powered off in between.

Next, he dialed 411 and asked for the direct line to Eighth District Police Station, Homicide Division.

CHIEF HOMICIDE DETECTIVE Alan Chevalier studied the details in his notepad, then reached for his coffee on the lobby counter of Hotel Josephine. He misjudged the position of the foam cup and instead knocked it over, spilling its contents all over the guest book he'd been going over.

The hotel's pretty owner, Josie Villefranche, hurried to sop up the mess with paper towels she pulled out from behind the counter.

"Thank you," he mumbled, taking a few sheets and wiping up what he could from his end. He realized that some of the hot liquid had splashed on his tie and he dabbed at that, as well.

Even as he did so, he caught himself staring with distaste at the stained piece of cloth, along with his wrinkled overcoat.

There was a time not so long ago that he had taken a certain amount of pride in his appearance. Even his co-workers had once jokingly named him "Best Dressed Detective" one year, complete with a plaque.

Now he couldn't seem to drum up the enthusiasm to take his things to the cleaners.

At thirty-six, he felt fifty-five. Of course, it didn't help that he knew he was completely responsible for the changes he'd undergone. When you bedded the captain's wife—no matter if they were estranged and lived in separate houses—it was only understandable that the boss would be a little pissed. Over the past ten months he'd been run through the wringer, suspended twice—once for a week, the next for a month—had pulled double duty and caught the blame for anything that went down wrong.

He knew he was being set up for dismissal. Knew it and couldn't do much about it but make sure everything he did on the job was aboveboard.

Still, the only thing that could make him forget about his professional life was drinking his way through his personal life.

He ran his fingers over the two-day stubble on his chin, his head reminding him of his binge the night before. Facing a murder investigation involving an FBI agent hostage when he had a hangover wasn't his idea of a good time and didn't bode well for the outcome.

He reached around the counter to toss the empty coffee cup into the wastebasket.

"Would you like another cup?" Josie asked.

Alan looked at her, finding it surprising that he hadn't thought to flirt with the very attractive young woman. But just as his professional life had taken a nosedive after his affair, so had his sex life. "Why? Do you see something I didn't ruin with this one?" he responded gruffly.

She smiled at him faintly, collected the paper towels, then disappeared through a doorway behind the counter.

He turned the page in his notebook, absently watching as the black body bag holding the recently deceased Miss Claire Laraway was carried down the stairs on a gurney.

He heard his cell phone chirp and had to look in three pockets before he finally found it.

"Chevalier," he said, dabbing at a spot he'd missed on his tie.

"This is Jean-Claude Lafitte and I am innocent of the crime I've been accused of."

Alan looked at his phone, the display indicating a blocked number, then moved it to his other ear as he also reached for his pen. "Mr. Lafitte, you haven't been accused of anything."

Yet. The word hung in the air.

A technicality really. And one dependent on the suspect's actual capture so he could be officially charged with the crime in question.

Alan motioned for his junior detective who stood nearby conversing with the medical examiner. "Mr. Lafitte, it would be better for everybody involved if you turned yourself in."

"Not until I prove my innocence."

In Alan's experience, if he were to believe ninety-nine percent of those he arrested, they were all innocent.

"And the agent?"

Silence.

But it told Alan what he'd needed to know. That Lafitte still held Akela Brooks.

"She's fine."

"I'm sure Akela's co-workers and family will be glad to know that, Mr. Lafitte."

He glanced at two of the agents in question who were deep in conversation near the door. Mentioning the hostage's first name and family served to remind the suspect that what he held was a human being with a name, not an inanimate object that wouldn't be missed should anything happen to her.

"Make sure you tell them she hasn't been harmed then," Lafitte said. "I'll be in contact when I find the evidence."

"What about—"

But Lafitte had already hung up.

Damn. Alan resisted the urge to smack his cell phone against the lobby desk a few times to vent his frustration. Too much was on the line now for him to play cat and mouse with a murder suspect.

5

AKELA STRAINED against her restraints as Lafitte
came back into the house. But his attention wasn't
on her. It seemed instead to be on the conversations
he'd had outside. Conversations she hadn't been
privy to because of the radio, which undoubtedly
he'd purposely turned on to keep her from over-
hearing him.

He glanced at her. For a moment she thought he
might have forgotten he'd taken her hostage, his
look of surprise was so genuine. He put his cell
phone down on the counter, turned down the radio, then strode across the room toward her.

Akela's every nerve ending went on alert. He had
yet to put another shirt on and was still barefoot, and
his casual attire made her feel more awkward still.
She wasn't used to people being so casual around her.
At her parents' house, no matter the heat, full dress
was expected, even at night and in the morning.

Lafitte reached for the chain around his neck

that held some sort of coin along with what she realized was the key to her cuffs. He pulled the simple silver chain over his head then unlocked the cuffs from her wrist.

He stood looking at her expectantly. Was he waiting for her to make a run for it?

"Didn't you say you had to go to the bathroom?"

Akela stopped rubbing her wrist. She'd forgotten she'd made the request. Part of the reason might be the subtle scent of spice that reached her nose, a scent that emanated from him and probably came from whatever soap he'd used during his shower.

She eyed his wide chest and the way his waist narrowed, then caught sight of the light sprinkling of hair below his navel that disappeared in a line down the front of his buttoned jeans.

"Um, yes."

He gestured toward the door in the corner. "It's over there."

Akela couldn't have moved fast enough. As soon as she closed the crude wood door after herself, she found out why he hadn't insisted on coming with her. The small room didn't boast any windows, and held only the bare necessities.

She quickly took care of business and started looking through the narrow medicine cabinet. Aspirin, rubbing alcohol, cotton swabs, shaving cream and a straight razor comprised the contents. She opened the razor, tested its sharpness, and then lifted the hem of her slip and slid it into the top elastic of her underpants. On the bottom shelf she found a needle bearing a short length of thread. She picked that up, as well, tested its strength, then fastened it just inside the cup of her bra.

There was a rap at the door and then it opened.

Akela started.

"I figured chances were better than good that you'd either be still on the commode or going through my medicine cabinet."

She stiffened and straightened her slip. "I have a headache." She grabbed the bottle of aspirin and shook out a couple of tablets.

"Not a phrase I hear often, although it seems to be a staple of most marriages."

Akela shot him a glance. "Are you talking from experience?"

He crossed his arms over his bare chest and leaned against the doorjamb. "*Non.* Never been tempted down that path."

He didn't seem in a hurry for her to leave. Then again, there really was no reason for him to be. She was essentially blocked in.

She took her time putting the aspirin onto her tongue one by one then following them up with water she scooped from the faucet into her mouth. Well water.

"You won't want to be doing that often," Lafitte said. "There's bottled water in the fridge."

She wiped droplets of the liquid in question from the side of her mouth then stood before him, indicating she wanted out. He stood solidly unmoving.

Akela was acutely aware of his proximity, standing tall and proud, regarding her openly. While he was tall, so was she.

He leaned closer, his nose mere millimeters away from her neck. He almost seemed to be smelling her.

"Mmm," he made a sound that was both intensely personal and heart-poundingly suggestive.

She suddenly couldn't draw a breath.

"Tell me, Akela—" her first name on his lips made her shiver "—have you ever not been in control of a situation?"

"No." The word came out as a harsh rasp.

He fingered a strand of her hair that had long escaped her twist, considering the dark strand with interest. She watched the shadows shift in his eyes, the dilating of his pupils, the shallowness of his breathing.

"I have," he said. "A long time ago. And I don't like that I'm not in control again now."

His other hand was at her hips, setting a tiny fire

there that nearly scorched her skin through the flimsy fabric of her slip. She caught her breath, her body yearning for exactly what he seemed to be offering with his touch.

All too abruptly he stepped back, holding up the straight blade he'd taken from under the elastic of her underpants without her even realizing it.

Akela swallowed hard, trying to rein in her runaway emotions.

"How did you know?"

He put the object into his own pocket. "Because if our roles had been reversed, it would have been the first thing I'd have gone for."

"You could have made things much easier by removing it before I went in."

"What would the fun have been in that?"

"Fun. Is that how you view this?"

He stared at her, the darkness back in his gaze. "I was speaking figuratively."

He moved away from the door, but didn't seem intent on refastening her to the bed. For that, at least, she was grateful. And she was careful not to make any quick moves that might cause him to change his mind.

"What do you do for a living?" she asked quietly, watching as he looked through the cupboards.

While he appeared unconcerned with her movements, she didn't kid herself into thinking that he didn't know exactly where she was and what her intentions were.

"I'm a business owner."

"What kind of business?"

His gaze narrowed on her face. "Why don't you sit down?"

He motioned toward a stool near the counter.

Akela slowly did as he asked, making sure her slip covered her and gauging the distance between him and her, and her and the door.

"You didn't answer my question."

"My brother and I began an airboat tour company in a nearby bayou and slowly expanded to include selling boats some years ago. I'm in the process of buying him out now."

His movements slowed as he took a couple of cans out of the cupboards, then a can of beans and a bag of rice. Another cupboard bore spices.

She was mildly surprised he was going to cook. Most men she knew couldn't boil an egg, much less knew their way around a kitchen. Her ex certainly hadn't known how to do anything beyond pour milk on top of store-bought cereal.

Lafitte appeared not only at home there in the small, makeshift kitchen, he looked somehow… right in his surroundings, despite the tension radiating from him in waves. She supposed it could be the way he moved, as if he really didn't have to think about what he was doing.

"What kind of boats?"

"Do you really want to know?"

She held his gaze, then admitted, "No."

"Didn't think so."

She couldn't help thinking that a man who had so much going on wouldn't jeopardize that by killing his lover.

He turned away from her to begin combining the ingredients in what she recognized was a crude, basic gumbo.

"How long you been an agent for the FBI?"

Akela pulled her gaze from where she'd been watching his back and the scar there. "Six years." She noticed there was a subtle red ring around her right wrist and gently rubbed it. "Do you have a prior criminal record?"

He didn't immediately answer, which she knew probably revealed more than what he might have said.

"Violent crime?" she asked.

"No."

"Then if you're innocent, why are you running?"

Now that was a question, wasn't it?

Claude was acutely aware of where Akela was

at all times. Not merely because he needed to keep tabs on her movements to prevent her escape, but because he seemed tuned into her on a level that bothered him because it had little to do with her as a hostage and everything to do with her as a woman. Yet it had only been a short time ago that he'd been in another woman's arms. But it wasn't the limited passage of time that disturbed him; rather it was the fact that that woman was now dead.

"As my brother and I are fond of saying, 'our mama didn't raise no fools.'"

"Why would turning yourself in make you a fool?"

"Because I would be putting my destiny in someone else's hands."

She seemed to give that some thought as she rubbed at the mark the cuffs had made on her wrist.

"You believe I did it? That I murdered Claire?" he asked point-blank.

"I don't know you well enough to say if you like corn on the cob."

That was honest.

"Besides, it's not part of my job to ascertain guilt or innocence."

"Whose is it if not yours?"

She squinted at him. "How do you mean?"

He'd combined the ingredients for the gumbo,

now it needed only to cook at a simmer. He turned and leaned against the counter, his arms crossed over his chest. He noticed the way her gaze kept trailing to his abs—which intrigued him. Seemed he wasn't the only one having trouble with keeping to their assigned roles. He couldn't seem to take his eyes off her, either. From the graceful sweep of her neck to the outline of her collarbone above her slip to the gentle swell of her breasts beneath the silky material.

"You, Agent Brooks, were the one who made the snap judgment that since I was at the wrong place at the wrong time, I must be a suspect."

"The hotel owner put you in the room with the girl."

"Sure. But I went out. Isn't it possible that it happened while I was gone?"

Her gaze skittered away. "That's not for me to decide."

"But you did decide. By pulling your gun on me and ordering me to freeze, you decided on the spot that I was guilty."

"I decided you were a suspect."

"With coffees and beignets? What do you suppose I planned to do with the extra? Feed them to a corpse?"

The expression on her face told him she'd seen others do worse.

Claude lifted his brows. He'd experienced much during his life. From the streets to the hills of Kosovo, he'd witnessed many things that had surprised him and changed his perception of the world, but nothing like what she was considering. "Are you that jaded?"

"I'm that educated."

Yes, perhaps that she was. But on all the wrong topics as far as he was concerned.

Oh, Claude didn't kid himself into thinking that there was no role for law enforcement. While his bayou roots dictated an eye for an eye, the injured party choosing revenge over reporting the incident to the police, he understood that things didn't work that way everywhere.

He also understood that those with badges were just as fallible as the next guy—his being under suspicion for killing Claire another glaring example of that.

"How was she killed?" he asked quietly.

That squinty-eyed look again. Claude frowned, realizing that she really did think he'd done it and he could virtually hear her ask, *I don't know. Why don't you tell me?*

"Her throat was slit."

Claude rubbed his face with his hands, remembering Claire's long, flawless neck. He could never have done something like that.

"And what is the FBI's interest in the case?"

She seemed to shift uncomfortably. "I was there on another matter."

"So your involvement is unofficial."

Her gray eyes flashed. "It had been until you took me hostage."

"Now I'm not only wanted for murder, but for kidnapping a federal agent."

"You're the one who got yourself into this mess."

"By making love to a beautiful woman?"

He reached into the fridge and took out two small bottles of water. He handed her one, noticing the way she automatically said thank you.

"You have to admit, Lafitte—"

"Call me Claude."

He knew she wouldn't. "Your taking me hostage does not reflect well on your innocence."

"So it makes me guilty."

"It makes you highly suspect."

He noted that as they spoke she eyed the door a few feet away.

"Ever been this deep into the bayous before?"

She blinked at him but didn't answer. He hadn't expected her to.

"Essentially your only way out is for me to take you out."

"I think you underestimate my abilities."

"I think you underestimate mine."

While physically, Claude came across his equal often, it had been a long, long time since he'd encountered a mental equal. But as he faced off with the lovely Agent Akela Brooks, he had little doubt that she was every bit his match.

And he had little doubt that she would somehow find her way out of the bayou if given the chance—with or without him.

But first, of course, she'd have to get past him.

"So tell me, Akela Brooks," he said quietly. "How do I go about proving my innocence?"

6

THREE HOURS LATER, Akela thought about her answer to Claude's question of how he could prove his innocence. Or rather she considered what had been, in essence, her nonanswer.

The cuffs clinked above her head and she had a crick in her neck from sitting upright for so long. After Lafitte had fed her a bowl of gumbo, he'd resecured her to the headboard then disappeared outside again, taking his phone with him. This time, however, he hadn't switched the radio on, leaving Akela alone with her thoughts and the sound of the bayou around her.

"Most suspects will try everything in their power to convince you of their innocence." A snippet of her training came back to her. *"And you must do everything in your power to ignore them."*

Something Akela had never had a problem with—until now.

It wasn't that Claude's…Lafitte's proclamations of innocence were any different from the others she'd encountered in her six-year career. Rather it was something she sensed rather than could explain, even though everything pointed to his guilt.

She supposed part of the reason was that he had yet to do her any harm. If, indeed, he was guilty of the crime, wouldn't he have done away with her by now? Wouldn't he have used her to try to escape the country?

Then again, if the crime was one of passion, then Lafitte wasn't a killer in the traditional sense of the word. He'd lost control in a fit of rage and committed manslaughter.

She moved to scratch her head with her bound hand, the cuffs stopping her. As she stared at the piece of unforgiving metal, she considered that perhaps the root of her dilemma was that no one had actually asked her the question Lafitte had: *"How do I go about proving my innocence?"*

She'd taken prelaw at Tulane, at the time not because she'd planned on being a law-enforcement officer, but because throughout her life, her mother had drilled into her the importance of two career choices: doctor or lawyer. She'd ultimately gone with lawyer mostly because she'd never done well when it came to blood.

One of the mock trials she'd participated in in her first year had involved a false accusation. She'd been assigned as part of the defense team. And the question had been pretty much what Claude had asked her: how did an innocent defendant prove he or she wasn't guilty?

"You can't disprove a negative. It's like asking you to prove God doesn't exist when there's no solid proof that he exists," she'd argued to her professor, finding the case a test of her patience and frustration.

She could still see the prof's knowing smile.

In the end, the mock defendant had been convicted of first-degree murder with recommendation of execution. Neither Akela nor her team had been able to disprove the negative.

So where did that leave Claude Lafitte? If he was indeed innocent, his prior record and his actions following the discovery of the murder scene would make him look guilty as sin.

Akela craned her neck to see out the window. From what she could tell from the light slanting through the thick vegetation, the sun was beginning its long descent toward the horizon. She couldn't see Claude or where he'd gone. It had been a long time since she'd heard anything other than the squawking of a bird and a slosh of water indicating that maybe an alligator or snake or something was nearby. Otherwise, nothing.

Using her free hand, she slid her fingers inside the neck of her slip and reached into the inside of her right bra cup for the needle she'd fastened there. It was almost sturdy enough not to bend, but after some work with her teeth and fingers, she managed to force a curve into the stubborn, narrow length of steel. She wiped her free hand against the bedding to rid it of moisture, then inserted the end of the needle into the lock on the cuffs. When her fingers slipped, she nearly lost the makeshift key. However, she quickly recovered it from where it was ready to bounce over the side of the bed.

Okay, maybe working on the cuff on her wrist wasn't a good idea. She switched her attention to the one attached to the headboard, which would allow her to use both hands. Holding the lock still, she worked the needle inside and felt her way around the mechanism. While the needle's strength had been a hindrance when she'd been trying to reshape, now it worked in her favor because it was strong enough to spring the lock—at least in theory.

Concentrating, she tried and tried again…and was finally rewarded with the sound of metal teeth giving.

She was free. She still had the cuffs secured to her right wrist, but she was free from the headboard. After pushing off the bed, she headed straight for the door and the porch beyond.

A sound at the side of the house reached her ears. Damn.

As quietly as possible, she collected her firearm from the barrel, gained silent access to the house and rushed for the bed. She shoved the gun under the pillow, then stared at the mattress. There was no way to pretend the cuffs were still attached to the headboard so she was forced to refasten them. Then she lay down to disguise her activities, hoping she was lying on top of the needle she'd tossed aside once she'd unlocked the cuffs.

She pretended to sleep.

CLAUDE STEPPED inside the house, feeling even worse now than he had before. He'd spent the past couple of hours on the phone with the attorney his brother had matched him up with. John Reginald had immediately contacted the NOPD and somberly admitted that things didn't look good for him—especially since he still held an FBI agent hostage.

He absently rubbed the back of his neck and considered the hostage in question. She was lying half on her back across the mattress, her legs pressed tightly together, her head turned his way, her eyes closed.

Claude grimaced. While Akela Brooks struck him as someone who could sleep anywhere, anytime if she put her mind to it, he doubted she would put her mind to it here. What intrigued him was why she was pretending to.

He stepped slowly closer to the bed, eyeing where the cuffs were still firmly attached to her wrist and to the headboard. At some point her chestnut hair had entirely escaped her professional twist, as if rebelling against the confining style. The damp bayou air had caused wisps to curl around her face, the rest of the shoulder-length tresses wavy and wild. The look it gave her was much different from the one he guessed she affected for work. Combined with the high color in her cheeks and the humidity dampening her skin, she looked like a sexy siren designed to drive man to madness.

Claude caught himself brushing the hair in question back from her face, his gaze lingering a little too long on her full, pouty lips. He checked the cuffs instead. When she didn't budge, he knew for sure she wasn't really asleep.

He stood silently for a long moment, trying to decide what to do, not just with her but the situation at large. It would be dark before long.

He sat down on the mattress, his gaze on her face. She didn't bat a lash.

Claude stretched out next to her, his side flush against hers. He figured the shock of his bare skin against her arm would at least send her jackknifing upward. To his surprise, she remained still.

What he hadn't factored into his little ruse was that he would end up affected by the touch of her skin. Despite the heat, she was cool and smooth. And she smelled good. Of something citrus. Not perfume; maybe lotion.

He heard her thick swallow.

Maybe she wasn't as unaffected as she appeared.

And given the darkness pressing in on him from all sides, he found he wanted to test boundaries better left alone.

AKELA WAS READY to jump straight out of her skin.

She forced herself to lie perfectly still, even though the part of her still capable of rational thought told her that she'd taken her sleep act too far, that what Lafitte was doing now was designed to rouse a reaction from her.

It was working, only not in the way she suspected he thought it might.

She knew the dangers inherent in such a situation. It had been in close confines—albeit completely different circumstances—that she'd convinced herself she'd been attracted to, and had fallen in love with, her ex. She and Dan had been on stakeout together, putting in double time as they tailed a suspected felon in a small town outside Oklahoma City. Their cover had been as young honeymooners on a cross-country road trip, so they'd stayed in the same motel room to perpetuate the roles.

Only their faked attraction to each other had turned quickly into the real thing.

It wasn't until after they'd married and had Daisy that they'd figured out that, aside from their jobs, they didn't have much in common. Not even passion.

Still, with Claude so close, Akela couldn't help thinking it had been so long since she'd allowed her body to take precedence over her head. Too long.

The bed beneath her was softer than anything she'd felt in a long, long time. While she'd been sitting on it for the past four hours, she hadn't noticed how soft it was until she was lying fully against it. The mattress nearly cocooned her in its layers of down, the high thread count sheets like silk against the exposed areas of her skin. The bedding smelled subtly like wildflowers. Narcissus? Orchids?

Then Claude had stretched out next to her and it was as though someone had struck a match and thrown it on top of her after dousing her with accelerant. Every nerve ending leaped to pulsating life. Her heart pounded an uneven staccato in her chest. She couldn't seem to draw a breath deeper than a shallow gasp. And her lower abdomen felt as if Claude had pressed a hot hand against it, eliciting a riot of longing in her.

Though they were touching, it wasn't in that way. Instead, he appeared to be going out of his way to make his actions seem casual, only her reaction to them was anything but.

This man had been with another woman that morning. That woman had died shortly thereafter, possibly at the hands of this man. None of this mattered to her. She only knew a burning desire to experience what he so openly seemed to be offering her.

Somewhere in the back of her mind she knew the wantonness of her thoughts should startle, if not scare her. She'd never been one to let go of her self-control. All decisions she made were in concert with her brain—which may be exactly the reason for the full-scale rebellion her body was staging now.

She felt something against her right nipple and gasped. No longer capable of pretending sleep, she threw her eyes open and stared at where Claude was leaning on one well-muscled arm, staring down at her, his expression sober. His other hand was above her chest, a finger having traced the edge of her slip.

"Ah, *cher,* I thought that might get your attention."

It did more than get her attention. Her nipples were bunched so tight they ached. And her stomach quivered from his attention.

But when she might or should have asked him to leave her be, tell him that molesting a hostage would only put him in hotter water, an unfamiliar voice whispered, almost pleaded, with her to give herself over to sensation just this once.

She licked her lips as her chest heaved from the difficulty she was having breathing.

Up this close and personal, she noticed how very attractive he was. Not in a Greek statue way. Rather in a wild Cajun way, with tousled hair, dark skin and an even darker allure that left her scanning his mouth and wondering what it would feel like to be kissed by him.

His finger grazed her skin again. Akela arched her back, pressing her breast into the palm of his hand and groaned, a response so outside her normal one that she was shocked—until Claude leaned over and showed her exactly what it would be like to kiss him.

Firm and probing and hungry, he slanted his mouth against hers, tentatively at first, as if giving her the option of pulling away, then more insistently, a low groan of his own filling her ears.

Long moments later he broke from her mouth and buried his nose along with the fingers of his right hand in her hair. "Ah, *poupée,* you present a temptation too strong for this mortal man to resist."

His words made her blood surge in her veins and hot wetness flood her inner thighs.

She'd never been an irresistible temptation to anyone. And the prospect that she was to him made her feel powerful despite the cuffs holding her captive.

She felt fingers against the sensitive skin of her inner knee and nearly came up off the bed, the jolt of electricity to her tender areas so intense she was sure he had set fire to her limbs. The hem of her slip slid up and she felt the humid air on her exposed underpants. She held his probing gaze, almost challenging him to take things further. Daring him.

She watched his gaze take her in from hair to bare toes, lingering on her crotch and her breasts where they strained against the material of her bra and slip.

"You're playing a very, very dangerous game, *ma catin.*"

Akela restlessly moistened her lips. "No more dangerous than the one you started when you took me captive."

His gaze flicked to hers where it stayed for a long heartbeat, touching her as thoroughly as any caress. "Ah, yes. Only I'm beginning to wonder who's keeping whom captive now."

She tugged on her wrist. "Release me and find out."

7

CLAUDE REALIZED he'd have to reassess his belief that beautiful FBI agent Akela Brooks was a woman not given to impulsive acts.

His gaze slid from the soft swell of her breasts, down to where the silky material of her slip skimmed her plain white panties, doing little to disguise the springy wedge of dark curls just beneath. A light sheen of sweat covered her supple skin and her chest rose and fell laboriously.

Another man might have viewed her suggestive request for freedom as a ploy toward escape. But if there was one thing Claude was an expert on, it was recognizing sexual need, and Akela's softly spoken challenge had nothing to do with finding a way out of the cabin and the bayou, and everything to do with showing him exactly what she promised.

Only Claude couldn't give in to the urge to unlock her cuffs, no matter how much he wanted to.

His legal position was too shaky right now. His avenues to clear himself were limited to the woman who was now looking up at him as if she wanted nothing more than to be kissed senseless.

But no matter how precarious his situation, and how vital his need to convince her of his innocence, he knew that's exactly what he was going to do.

Drawing his fingers up her hip and over her side, at her quick intake of breath, he pressed his mouth against hers. And he was rewarded with her arching up toward him, her cuffs clanking, her body hot and supple.

His mama had been fond of saying that her brand of Cajun cooking could put the heat in anyone's veins. That the hot spices didn't just tease the tongue, they wove their way through the bloodstream, making the person restless and yearning for an unnamable something.

Of course, Olivie Lafitte also said that excusing yourself for bad behavior was inexcusable.

Claude felt Akela's finger at the side of his neck, then her touch trailed down over his bare arm to his chest. She pressed her damp palm against his flat nipple, her eyes fluttering slightly open to watch his response to her bold move. Normally it would have taken a whole helluva lot more than a touch north of the snap on his jeans to do it for him. But her tentative touch and the warm quicksilver of her eyes combined to make him feel as if he'd been sucker punched.

And that, more than anything, should have warned him to be careful before pushing ahead. But he couldn't seem to help himself, could no sooner stop what was happening between them than he could the beating of his own heart.

He kissed her as his palm slid down the fluid material of her slip. The heel of his hand hesitated against her pelvis. And she bucked against his touch like a woman gone mad with desire.

Dear Lord…

She rolled over on top of him, her knees on either side of his hips, putting her in direct contact with his straining arousal. He closed his eyes and reveled in the myriad sensations caused by the move.

Then he heard an ominous click and he looked up to find himself staring down the muzzle of an all-too-familiar gun. Holding it was Akela, looking tousled and sexy as hell—and very much in control.

She licked her lips. "I told you when the gun was back in my hands, we were going to have that conversation again."

EVEN AS AKELA'S THIGHS burned where they squeezed his hips, his powerful erection pressing against her delicates, she aimed her firearm. The metal was heavy in her free hand but she was well trained in the art of one-hand shooting. Besides, at this close range she couldn't miss.

Claude's green eyes took her in. "Ah, I wondered what you were hiding when I came in and you were pretending to be asleep."

"Unlock the cuffs."

Akela watched as he reached for the chain around his neck. She backed up a hair to give him the room he needed to ensure he couldn't take the gun. Then she heard the teeth from her cuffs give as Claude released the metal shackle from her wrist.

She immediately grasped the gun in both hands.

Claude lay back and considered her.

"Do it," he said quietly.

Akela's throat tightened. She hadn't retrieved the firearm in order to kill him. She'd merely been trying to regain her freedom.

"Go ahead, shoot. The way things look, I'm a dead man, anyway."

She blinked at him, thinking he couldn't be serious.

She began to climb off him.

That's when he made his move. He took advantage of her being off balance and grasped her wrists, forcing the muzzle of the gun away from him at the same time he rolled her over, his body pinning her to the bed, his hips solidly between her legs. The gun was above her head, held there by his strong hands. But he didn't appear interested in trying to take it from her. Rather he was staring at her as if in disappointment.

For the life of her, Akela couldn't figure out why he would be disappointed.

He rolled off her and pushed from the bed. Then he held his hand out to her. "I wasn't going to do this until the sun goes down, but I can see I no longer have a choice."

Akela swallowed hard, leaving her hands and the gun above her head. "Do what?"

He didn't say anything.

Dropping the gun to her side, she took his hand with her free one and he hauled her from the bed.

"Gather your things and come on."

Akela felt oddly out of sorts as she watched him turn and walk through the door. Keeping a tight grip on her gun, she quickly put her skirt and blouse back on, barely buttoning the top before joining him where he stood on the porch staring out at the bayou.

Shadows were lengthening and the autumn sunlight gave the mist-heavy air a purplish, surreal tint. A light breeze teased Spanish moss. The tall cypresses spoke to each other.

"You grew up here?"

Akela was somewhat surprised to hear her voice ask the question as she tucked her gun back into the holster inside her jacket. She was surprised further that she wanted to know the answer to it.

"Mmm. My brother and I were raised by our mother."

"And your father?"

She felt his gaze on her and blinked to find him staring at her while he slowly fastened the buttons on his denim shirt. "Could have been one of three men, if you believed the rumors."

"The truth?"

"He was a shopkeeper on the outskirts of the bayou who was already spoken for."

"Married?"

"Yes."

In the social circle in which Akela had been raised, being someone's bastard child was tantamount to death. At least if the situation wasn't socially remedied. The way her mother told it, if a woman in their social circle was in trouble, in the kind of situation Claude's mother had been in, there was always the son of a congressman whose sexual orientation was in question who could pose as a perfectly good substitute. And the child himself…well, he'd never have to know of his true parentage.

Such incidents happened all the time.

And in Claude's mother's case, it might have been an older, maybe widowed man from another part of the bayou who could have been a companion to her, a father of sorts to her sons. But she hadn't chosen that route.

Strangely, Claude didn't appear to be apologizing for his mother's behavior. He was merely stating fact.

"Did you know him growing up?"

"My father? No. He died when I was three. I have no memory of him. Not that I would have even if he had survived."

She nodded. Of course not. The woman would have raised her bastard son on her own, allowing for the gossiping around her, never asking for anything from the man who had fathered the child.

Akela wasn't sure which way was worse: her own mother's or Claude's mother's.

"Come."

He took her hand and led her down the steps then around the house. They'd walked for some time before he reached the car he'd used to drive her out there.

She asked, "Aren't you afraid I'll remember the way?"

Claude looked at her, then handed her into the passenger's seat. "If you can remember your way back here, then I deserve to be found."

She looked around even as he climbed in next to her and started the car.

"So you're letting me go, then," she said quietly.

"So I'm letting you go, then."

Akela wasn't entirely sure how she felt about that. A few short hours ago she would have been elated. Would have been planning exactly what she would do and how she might go about apprehending the man who had taken her prisoner.

Now she could only stare out at the sights around her, the bayou, the swamps, listening to the utter quietness as Claude turned the car around and drove in the direction of the nearest highway, seemingly unconcerned with her taking mental notes on their whereabouts.

She feared the reason for her ambivalence was that she didn't want him to let her go. Not yet.

Somehow she felt as if the past few hours had existed as time outside of time. The bayou and perhaps even Claude himself had worked their way under her skin. And, she discovered, she was worried about what would happen from there. Worried about Claude. Worried that if her instincts were right, and he hadn't killed Claire Laraway, that he would never be able to prove it.

She stared at his hands where they gripped the steering wheel. Thick, long and calloused, they seemed incapable of touching her as gently as they had. She rested her own hand against the side of her neck, noting the heaviness of her pulse there. She had the feeling that Claude's hands weren't all that unlike the man himself. Hardened by a difficult upbringing, he still had a gentleness that touched her on a level she had been helpless to protect herself against. And she couldn't help thinking that somehow her short time with Claude Lafitte had changed her, possibly forever.

"Agent Brooks, Agent Brooks! Officials report their fear that the suspect sexually mistreated you. Any comment?"

The following morning Akela ducked inside the front doors of Eighth District Police Station, keeping her chin down, her eyes straight ahead, no matter how much she wanted to refute the allegations that had swirled around her ever since Jean-Claude

Lafitte had set her free a block away from where he'd taken her prisoner the night before.

The chaos that had ensued immediately afterward was enough to make anyone sick. From accusations that she'd had a prior connection to the "modern-day pirate," to stories that she'd actually helped him escape, the city's rumor mills were running overtime with decadent possibilities. One morning-radio show personality had actually begun running a verbal serialization of the ordeal, providing a fictional account of what might have happened for entertainment value alone.

But, of course, no one but she and Claude really knew what had happened. Nothing.

Akela's cheeks burned in the cold air-conditioning as she climbed the stairs to the second floor. Well, almost nothing had happened.

Twelve hours had passed since Claude had handed her out of the car as easily as if they'd gone on a date, then lightly kissed her temple, his fingers hot against her skin. And she had left her gun in her holster, not even attempting to place the fugitive under arrest.

"You should surrender yourself to authorities," she'd whispered even as her eyelids had fluttered closed under the tenderness of his chaste kiss.

"I will, *chere.* But not yet. Not yet."

An NOPD detective waved a morning paper at her as she entered the second-floor bull pen room. "Says here you're due to give birth to Lafitte's love child in nine months."

Akela stared at him. "I'm sure it also says in there that aliens founded our fair city and the time clock is ticking on its destruction."

"How did you know?"

A few detectives chuckled as she continued on toward the glassed office at the end of the large room. She rapped briefly before letting herself in, the cast of characters inside ones she'd gotten used to since last night.

Chief Detective Lieutenant Alan Chevalier sat behind his desk, his feet crossed on top, his fingers tented against the wrinkled front of his shirt.

"Agent Brooks," the man in question said, "I didn't expect to see you in again so soon."

She ignored the sarcasm in his voice. Most local law-enforcement agencies didn't appreciate federal involvement in any case, much less one as highly visible as this one. It was a territorial thing. In her case, however, she was there strictly in an observational capacity. Her own superior had released her from duty so she could assist in the apprehension of the fugitive that had bruised the FBI's image by taking one of their own hostage.

She asked, "Have you gotten an address on the Lafitte house?"

"In the bayou? No."

She took out a map from the inside pocket of her jacket. "I put my head together with a geologist at the field office. Here's a rough outline of what I think we're looking at."

"Rough outline?"

"Mmm. A map. I already have a native lined up to drive us out there—or should I say, airboat us out there."

"Agent Brooks, I wasn't aware that the FBI had taken over control of this case."

"We haven't."

Chevalier slowly removed his feet from his desktop, his gaze steady on her. "Then I'd appreciate you not trying to take control."

She held his gaze. "Are you interested in catching Lafitte or not?"

She noticed a tick in his jaw. "Of course."

"Then act like it."

Chevalier sat forward, obviously insulted, which helped none of them at all.

Akela took a deep breath. This wasn't the first time she'd been placed in the position of selling an idea. She just hadn't thought she'd have to here. "Look, ever since your men picked me up last night outside the hotel, you've been treating me like I'm the suspect, behavior I'm not very happy with. And now you want to try to lock me out of any attempt to apprehend a man who held me captive for six hours."

"The last place Lafitte would go back to is the bayou," Chevalier argued.

"Oh, yes? Well did that little pearl of wisdom form before or after I was released last night?"

Alan stared at her.

"Look, the last thing I want to do is undermine your investigation, Chevalier. But unless you have any other leads you're working on—"

"Actually, we do."

Akela crossed her arms and waited.

"I've been talking with Lafitte's attorney. Lafitte is about to turn himself over to authorities as we speak."

Akela remembered the bits of conversation she'd overheard yesterday.

"He's buying himself more time," she said.

"Time for what? To make a run for it? Even you said you don't think he has plans to leave town."

"Does that mean we shouldn't try to apprehend him?"

"Agent Brooks, I don't know where you're from, but wherever it is, obviously things work a little differently there than here. Here in NO, we're a little more civilized."

"You mean lazy."

One of the plainclothes officers nearer the door held up a paper and cleared his throat. "Brooks is from NO, Lieutenant."

Alan seemed to stare at her more closely and she returned his attention. Then, breaking her gaze away, she gathered her map, folded it, then headed for the door.

"Where are you going?" Chevalier asked.

"Out there on my own."

"I'm the one in charge of this case."

"Then do something to solve it."

8

AKELA DIDN'T LIKE going over others' heads. It didn't bode well for any working relationship. People tended to be a little pissed when their authority was questioned then stepped on.

But she hadn't been able to help herself. It was more than her career on the line. With every off-color question she was asked by reporters, every speculative glance she received from her co-workers and superiors, and after sitting across the table from her mother's accusatory face that morning, she needed to clear her name, and she needed to do it *now*.

If her deep-seated desire also had anything to do with her own momentary flash of weakness when it came to Claude Lafitte, that was between her and the man in question.

She pressed her hand to the base of her throat, aware of the heat there. Though she wished she could blame that on the weather, she knew it had more to do with her awareness that, while Lafitte hadn't ravaged her as everyone suspected, she'd wanted him to ravage her. A man suspected of killing his lover. A man who had been in the arms of that same lover mere hours before he'd kissed Akela. But the fact remained that she'd wanted him to do much more.

The airboat sped through the bayous, sending spray up into her face, the sound of the large, propelling fan deafening. There were two boats and she was on the first one, her navy-blue slacks damp, her flak jacket heavy over her navy cotton T-shirt. No sooner had she made the threat to Chevalier than they were on the boats she'd secured, speeding toward a spot on the map where she hoped they would find Lafitte.

Nearby an alligator easily as long as the boat slid back into the water from where it had been sunning itself on the shore, the ripples it made minimal. Akela checked her firearm, resecured her mobile radio transmitter on her shoulder then looked at her watch. They'd agreed to cut the engines some five minutes away from the rendezvous point, not wanting to announce their approach to everyone within a twenty-mile radius. And that point was coming up….

The driver downshifted the engine and the boat

slowed to an easy coast on the shallow green water. Next to them, the second boat did the same.

There were ten members of the NOPD all told. Five on her airboat, five on the other. All of them checked their weapons, none of them saying anything. Everything had already been said. They would split up into two teams on the other side of the narrow peninsula, one approaching the cabin from the north, the other from the south. She knew a third team was approaching via the only road into and out of this area of the bayou—the same road Claude had used to take her there the day before.

Had it really only been a day since she'd lain cuffed to his headboard listening to the sounds of the bayou, wanting a man she'd had no business wanting? The experience was so outside anything she could compare it to that she found it almost easier to imagine it a dream—a very detailed, vivid dream that still made her limbs go limp and yearning pool in her abdomen.

"Two minutes out," the boat captain said to her.

She nodded and indicated that the other boat should split off. She pulled a shotgun from where she'd secured it against the low side of the boat and cocked it, the sound loud and isolated in the comparative silence. A flock of vultures set off from a stand of trees, cawing in warning. She ignored them even as she searched for a landmark she might recognize.

There. To her right she watched three dark sedans speed down the road toward Lafitte's cabin. There would be no out for him now—at least not through conventional routes. And with their two boats, an escape via the bayou would be cut off, as well.

The airboat hit the side of a grassy knoll and she bolted onto the soft earth, the other men following behind her. She led the way through thick vegetation, her booted feet hitting soggy patches of land here and there until finally she burst through the brush and stood off to the west of the cottage where Lafitte had held her captive the day before.

On the other side, the other team was doing the same, the third team coming up from behind the cabin via the road.

Akela held up her fingers and counted down from three, then ran for the porch, taking the stairs two steps at a time until she flanked the right side of the door, another officer flanking the other. She didn't bother with niceties. Instead she opened the screen door, the other officer kicked in the wood door and they both entered, training their sights on the interior.

The empty interior.

Damn.

She quickly searched inside.

"House secured. Spread out and search the area," Akela said into her radio.

She heard footsteps outside then Chevalier was moving inside the house wearing his trademark rumpled trenchcoat and lighting a cigarette. "You won't find him."

Akela resisted the urge to point her shotgun at him, handing it off to a fellow officer instead. "If I didn't know better, Lieutenant, I'd say you're privy to information the rest of us aren't."

He smiled at her. "Not privy. Just mindful of." He stepped toward the bed in the corner and considered the empty cuffs still fastened to the headboard. He raised a brow at her. "This where he held you?"

Akela didn't answer. She'd already told him what had gone down the day before. Three times. She wasn't about to tell him again.

Besides, just looking at that bed made her remember feelings she'd be better off forgetting—for good.

The scent of cigarette smoke reached her nose and she stepped out of the cloud.

"If we'd come last night as I wanted, we might have caught him," she said, stepping back outside.

"If we'd come last night, we would have gotten lost," Chevalier said, following her.

"If I recall, that wasn't your argument then."

He looked at her. "No. It wasn't."

Essentially his argument had been that she was emotionally overwrought and wouldn't have been able to remember where Lafitte had taken her. So he'd told her to go home and get some rest—rest she had yet to get.

Akela walked the perimeter of the house back to the shower. She didn't dislike Chevalier. While he was a chauvinist pain in the ass, he had been very adept at his job judging by the framed accolades on his wall, and what others had said about him. At least up until recently. And while with his sarcasm he made it seem he didn't like her, she knew that he held a grudging respect for her and her position. And once he'd agreed to the raid, she hadn't heard a single smart-ass remark. Well, at least until they'd figured out Lafitte wasn't there.

Of course, it didn't pass her notice that he was in some sort of trouble with the higher-ups at his station or else she would have had a more difficult fight on her hands when she'd gone in there this morning.

"The deed?" she asked when she'd come back around, directing the question at Chevalier where he stood with a few of his men.

"None on record," he said. "There are some places out here that aren't listed in any books yet."

So essentially this place didn't exist. There was no way to tie it in any official way to Lafitte.

Something shone in her eyes, briefly blinding her. She held her hand to her brow and squinted out across the bayou. The three teams were gathering back at the cabin. Akela started in the direction of the swamp, keeping her gaze fixed on the spot where she swore she'd seen the flash.

CLAUDE LIFTED the binoculars again, staring at the woman some two hundred yards away with what he told himself was little more than detached interest. Problem was, not even he was having any of it. He felt…well, almost proud, if truth be told. He was proud Agent Akela Brooks had not only remembered where the old cabin was but that she had brought enough firepower along to bring down a small town.

Akela seemed to look directly at him.

Claude dropped the binoculars and squinted in her direction. Of course she couldn't see him. But the way her gaze had slammed into his through the glass made him believe for half a second that she had.

He fished for his cell phone and called a number he'd programmed in, then moved the binoculars back to his eyes. He watched Akela search for her cell. She apparently didn't recognize the number and for a moment he thought she might ignore the incoming call. Then she pressed the button and said, "Hello?" her gaze still scanning the area around where Claude hid.

"You found me."

He watched her eyes go round. The police detective was looking at her curiously but rather than indicate that she had him on the line, she turned and walked away from the throng of police. "Obviously I didn't find you, or else I'd be looking at you right now. And you'd be the one wearing handcuffs this time."

Claude chuckled softly, finding her actions more interesting than her words. Why hadn't she let on to her co-workers that she had him on the line? That he was obviously nearby?

"Can you see me?" she asked.

"I can see you."

"So why don't you come out and give yourself up?"

It was more of a comment than a question. Probably because they both knew there would be no giving up of anything. At least not yet. Not until Claude could prove his innocence.

"I can't," he said. "Why don't you give up looking for me?"

He watched as she lifted her chin and smiled as

if she suspected he was looking at her head-on and wanted him to see her. "I can't."

"So where does that leave us?"

"Pretty much at a stalemate."

"Mmm."

She turned to look at the cabin. "This isn't your place, is it?"

"Nope."

"But you do have one nearby."

"Yes."

She scanned the area around her.

"You could stay behind alone and I'll show it to you."

"Why? So you can take me hostage again?"

"No, so we can continue what we started yesterday. But this time, as equals."

He could have sworn he saw her shiver.

"I think the scales would still be a bit unbalanced."

"Only because you want to arrest me."

She didn't say anything.

"You could try to help me prove my innocence."

He watched her eyes as they squinted, filled with what he could only guess was wariness.

"That's why I can't give myself up."

"Yet."

"Yes, yet."

"Why?"

"Because not even you believe in my innocence."

"I don't know you."

"I think you know me better than either of us is willing to admit."

"Agent Brooks?"

He watched as the detective in the overcoat came up behind her. She raised a hand to ward him off.

"If I stay?"

If she stayed…

Claude thought of the dangerous game they'd begun the day before. Could still taste the sweetness of her flesh on his tongue. Feel her thighs gripping his hips.

"You'll have to be the judge of that."

He watched as she slapped her phone closed then turned to face the detective.

Claude closed his own phone, then drifted back farther into the bayou shadows. While he'd correctly read Akela's attraction to him, he hadn't expected her to find her way back to the cabin so easily. He'd have to remember not to underestimate her from there on out.

He watched as the three teams of officers began to disperse, two of them with the airboats, the other backtracking toward the road. He suspected they might leave someone behind. He was mildly surprised when it was Akela.

AKELA UNFASTENED the pulls on her flak jacket, then let the heavy protective vest hang from her shoulders, her T-shirt underneath damp. The last of her support team had left about fifteen minutes ago, leaving her behind on her request. Sitting on the porch's wood steps, she scanned the surrounding area, hoping Lafitte had watched them go, hoping even more that he'd noticed she had stayed.

She didn't miss the irony of her actions. She'd come out here with every intention of bringing him into custody, where she felt he'd be safer. With her on the job, she wouldn't have to worry about one of Chevalier's rookies spooking and squeezing a shot at Claude.

She should have known it wouldn't be that easy. Should have suspected it would take more than a few clever maneuvers to arrest the ex-marine.

She'd practically memorized his background check. Knew the details of his arrest at nineteen when he'd been found bleeding from a stab wound in the back—which explained the scar—and left for dead when a black-market sale of small arms had gone bad. He'd been the seller, and apparently the buyer had decided he didn't want to pay for what Claude had stolen. It had been his first offense, during a time when the laws weren't as unforgiving as they were now, so the judge had given him a choice: prison or a stint in the military.

He'd chosen the military. Where he'd not only served, but served well. He'd worked his way up to a prime position in Elite Forces, going above and beyond in his duty as scout and sniper in both Kosovo and Somalia. The marines had tried to talk him into staying when his time was up, but he'd taken his honorable discharge, then gone into business with his older brother, buying scrapped watercraft, rebuilding the engines, then reselling them at triple the price. The business had grown over the years to include popular bayou airboat tours and now dealt in new as well as used and refurbished boats.

It was that business that Claude was now in the process of buying from his brother, a deal that would undoubtedly fall through if Claude couldn't clear his name. And the only way she felt he could do that was by turning himself over to authorities.

She glanced at her watch then ran the back of her hand across her brow. It was even hotter today than it had been yesterday, if that was possible. The very air around her seemed to liquefy. The scent of green and decay filled her nose. And her heart beat so thickly she wasn't all that convinced that she was physically sound. Obviously, her psychological soundness was already in question.

She shrugged out of the jacket and dropped it with a dull thunk to the wood steps. There wasn't anything she could do about the pants but roll them up a few times, but she left her boots on.

"Waiting for someone?"

The words came from the porch behind her. She stiffened a bit, but only because, despite everything, Lafitte had managed to get the jump on her.

She released the bullet loaded into her automatic with a quick shift of the mechanism, then put the firearm back into the holster attached to her flak jacket.

"You could say that," she said.

She heard footsteps and scooted over on the stairs so he could pass. Instead he took a seat next to her. Akela squinted at him, taking in the width of his biceps, the firmness of his thighs in his jeans.

"Some might think that a little dangerous."

She glanced at where her firearm was well within reach for both of them. "Yes, they might."

"But you don't."

"No, I don't."

She felt his finger on the hair above her right ear. Then she felt his breath. "Maybe you should, *chere.*"

9

SHE SMELLED LIKE ORANGES. Oranges, for God's sake. Claude leaned closer, breathing in the scent of her.

He almost hadn't allowed himself to believe his luck when he'd watched the rest of the three teams leave her behind. She'd obviously come out loaded for bear. Yet she hadn't hesitated to stay behind alone.

"I don't get you, Brooks," he said quietly.

Her full mouth turned up in a smile. "I'm not getting myself much lately, either."

He liked that. The fact that she could be honest without fear that he'd somehow use the information against her.

"Aren't you worried what your detective friends will think of your staying behind alone?"

"They probably think I'm insane."

"And your answer to that would be?"

"That maybe I am." She absently scratched her arm under the sleeve of her T-shirt, as if her skin suddenly itched all over. "I just knew that even if we stuck around here all day, we wouldn't have caught you. And since you're not willing to give yourself up yet…"

Yet.

Claude's mind caught and held on the small but important word. Yet. They both understood that eventually he would give himself up. But not until he had the goods with which to exonerate himself.

She shrugged. "I don't know. I suppose there are plenty of other ways I could have chosen to spend the day."

"Yes, but how many of them include conversing with a known criminal?"

"I wouldn't say you were a known criminal. You're a suspected murderer."

Claude flinched, not finding the description any better. "Who's on the lam."

She looked at him. "Maybe I stayed behind so I could convince you to surrender to me."

Had a definite ring to it, his surrendering to her. Only he suspected they were thinking of two different kinds of surrender. She was talking about jail cells and Miranda rights, while he would like to think her words had more to do with the bed in the cabin behind them and the cuffs that were still attached to the headboard.

"I think we could work out the terms of my surrender," he said, running the back of his index finger along the outer part of her arm. He watched her shiver in response.

"Oh?"

"Mmm. Say I put my hands up right now and let you have your way with me?"

"Well, I'd, um, probably have to handcuff you to something until one of the airboats returns to get me."

"And will they be doing that? Returning to get you?"

"Yes. In an hour."

"Ah."

Her expression seemed to indicate she felt the same way.

"There's a lot we can accomplish in an hour."

"Fifty-nine minutes."

He scanned her pretty features.

"All I need is a minute."

"A little quick, isn't it?"

"There's nothing quick about what I do."

She seemed to think on that one, her pupils dilating in her silver irises. "But that would mean I'd have to surrender to you," she said.

He gave her a lazy, purely suggestive grin and shrugged. "Well, I figure that's all I've got since you don't seem to be taking me up on my offer to surrender to you...."

She picked up her firearm and cocked it again.

He twisted it out of her fingers. "How about we leave guns out of it this time?"

"And handcuffs?"

"Your call."

She stared at him for a long time then leaned in and kissed him, slowly, lingeringly, as if she hadn't been able to help herself. And Claude was helpless to do anything but watch the fine picture she made, this FBI agent, this beautiful woman, with her wild brown hair pulled back into a French braid, her eyes wide and full of passion and want.

"Cuffs," she said.

She stood up, twisting his arm in a way that gave him the option of either getting up or listening to his bone snap in two. He chuckled, stumbling up the stairs toward the door.

The police before them had left the door open so he walked straight inside then caught himself when she shoved him toward the bed none too delicately. He'd turned around to sit when she launched herself across the bed on top of him, clutching at his T-shirt, scrambling to free herself of her own. Claude groaned as he filled his fingers with her sweet flesh.

He'd thought of this one moment no fewer than a dozen times in the past hours, ever since he'd taken her from this very bed, driven her into the city and let her go.

He heard her zipper and watched as she kicked off her boots then shimmied out of her slacks, leaving nothing but a pair of red silky underwear and a white bra. He slid the tip of his index finger under one of the cups of her bra, seeking for and finding her engorged nipple. She moaned, tossing her head back even when he fastened his mouth over her through the material and suckled. She slid against him, her skin damp against his, her sex skimming over the throbbing proof of his own need for her.

Akela Brooks was supple everywhere a woman was supposed to be and soft everywhere a man could want. Her breasts weren't overly large, but they weren't small, either, fitting nicely into his palms and his mouth.

And her bottom…*mon Dieu*…

He slid his fingers up the swell of flesh in question, dipping the tips under the elastic until his palms were filled with her lush buttocks. He kneaded the firm flesh, then parted them. She made a low sound as her fingers grasped his right arm and then trailed down to the hand, which she pulled above his head. He heard metal against metal as she fastened the cold cuff around his wrist, her eyes filled with need and challenge and something he couldn't quite identify.

She kissed him almost roughly. "Whatever happens in this room stays in this room."

He could deal with those terms. Making whatever was happening between them a matter of public record probably wouldn't help either one of them.

Then again, at the moment he might possibly agree to just about anything so long as he could feel her tight, wet womanhood surrounding him.

He jutted his hips upward, forcing a meeting between his jean-covered erection and the apex of her thighs. She sat up and rubbed her silk-covered mound over him, forcing him to tense against the sensations that swelled within him. Reaching down, she slowly undid the buttons at his fly, then slid down his legs and freed him of the heavy denim. If she was surprised he didn't wear briefs, she didn't indicate. She merely climbed her way back up his legs, flicking her tongue over his hair-covered thighs, then up farther to tease the skin around his throbbing arousal. Meeting his gaze, she drew her long, pink tongue up the length of his erection. Claude's hips bucked instinctively and she smiled, fingering the bead of moisture on the knob. Then she set about tasting him more thoroughly.

He closed his eyes and yanked against the cuffs, needing to touch her. He'd have to make do with his left hand. He grasped her under the arm and hauled her up so they were face-to-face and kissed her hungrily; at the same time he sought the back catch to her bra. The stretchy fabric gave and her breasts sprang free. He wasted no time fastening his mouth over her right nipple, sucking deeply.

Akela gasped, stretching her head back as she switched his attention to her other breast, then back again, seemingly unable to get enough. He curved his hand around her back and down to grasp her bottom, then positioned her so that only her panties separated his flesh from hers.

He watched her lick her lips restlessly. "Do you have…anything?"

Claude grinned wickedly. "How do you mean?"

Her answer was a provocative rub against him. "In my jeans pocket."

She reached for his discarded pants and fished in his pockets until she came up with a foil-wrapped packet. She made quick work of opening it then held it out to him.

"You're going to have to do it." He yanked on the cuffs for emphasis.

He was curious as to her hesitation. Up until that moment she'd been bold bravado and wanton sex kitten. Now she looked between the condom and his hard-on as if she didn't know how the two fit together.

Claude gently grasped the hand holding the rubber and moved it to his turgid flesh. He fitted the condom over the top, then guided her fingers to smooth it down the length of him. When she reached the root, she gave a squeeze that made him grit his teeth against coming.

He grasped the crotch of her panties and tugged hard, listening to her gasp as the material gave, baring her to his hungry gaze. She was as beautiful as he knew she would be. Her curls were neat and springy, pink flesh peeking out. She scooted up so that she was directly above him and he guided the tip of his erection between her slick folds, reveling in the hot feel of her against him. She jerked her hips, trying to force penetration. He denied her the immediate satisfaction, instead moving his head to the top of her shallow channel, finding the bit of erect flesh there and rubbing himself against it. As a result, he was rewarded with her deep shudder.

Also as a result, she wrested control of his manhood to reposition him, and then she slid slowly down his long length until he was completely filling her.

He watched her shivering breasts, her hard nipples, her impossibly straight back, as she took him in. Then she rocked against him, sliding back and forth, her deep-throated moan nearly ending it for him.

Claude found few things more pleasurable than having a beautiful woman sitting astride him, riding him. But Akela Brooks was more than just another beautiful woman. What she represented, what her surrender to him and to her desires symbolized, brought a uniqueness to their lovemaking that fascinated him. He watched her expressive face. Saw the sweat shimmering on her elongated neck. Took in the sheer bliss on her pretty face. And felt as though he'd been transported somehow, to a place he hadn't visited in a long, long time—*if* he'd ever been there before at all.

He grasped her hip with his free hand, stilling her so he could thrust deeply upward. Her moan wrapped around him and she shifted to give him better access. He bucked up again, and yet again, her slick womanhood feeling so damn good around him he wanted to burst.

And when he did finally give in to that urge long minutes later, he felt that he'd been changed in some irrevocable, mysterious way.

AKELA COULDN'T HAVE felt more outside herself had she been wearing someone else's skin. She lay against the cool sheets, her body heated, her muscles sated, the mere act of trying to catch her breath enough to occupy her entire energy reserve.

She'd never felt so thoroughly sexed and so utterly spent.

She lazily ran her fingernails against Claude's back, over the puckered scar there near his buttocks, the sheen of sweat on his skin. Her sex throbbed with a life of its own. Her breasts were so tight she was filled with the urge to cry out from the sensitivity of them.

Had she really just spent the past forty-five minutes having sex with a man wanted for murder? Only sex seemed such an inadequate word somehow. What she and Claude had shared transcended the mere physical coming together of two people.

Or did it?

She pushed her damp hair back from her face and considered the fan working in lazy circles on the ceiling. She couldn't say, really. Oh, she'd had sex before—with three different men over a period of ten years. But none of those experiences had left her with the bone weariness she now felt. And none had left her wanting more when by all rights she should be holding up her hands and swearing surrender.

She felt Claude's fingers on the swollen folds of slippery flesh between her legs. She threw her head back and moaned, sure she couldn't stand another moment…certain that she'd go crazy if he didn't take her again right that minute.

"Your boat should be returning for you anytime," he murmured, sliding a finger through her shallow channel then tweaking her hooded flesh.

"Screw my ride."

"But won't they come looking for you?"

"I told them to wait for me at the junction five minutes away."

"And if you're not there within an acceptable amount of time?"

She wanted to groan for an entirely different reason. "They'll come looking for me."

He didn't need to respond. They both knew very clearly what that meant.

Akela forced herself to roll up to a sitting position.

"You could always call and cancel the ride."

She looked at him over her bare shoulder. "And tell them what? That I ran into the suspect and I'm now the one holding him hostage, only I want some more time alone with him?"

He slid his hand down the center of her back. "That might work."

"Does that mean you intend to turn yourself in?"

The hand disappeared.

"That's what I thought."

The bedsprings creaked as he sat up on the opposite side of the bed. She'd freed him from the handcuffs some time ago and they clanked against the top of the bed.

Akela couldn't believe the contrast they made. Her the FBI agent, good girl. Him the Cajun fugitive, the ultimate bad boy. Yet when they came together today they did so as equals.

"So where do we go from here?" she asked quietly, fastening her bra then pulling her T-shirt back over her breasts.

"Square one."

"I think we long surpassed that."

"Mmm. Maybe you're right."

He started to dress even as she finished, doing up the laces of her boots.

"I guess I head back to the city," he said.

Akela's heart skipped a beat.

The hotel aside, she'd always thought of him in terms of the bayou, not the city, even though she knew he had an apartment not far from where her parents lived in the Garden District.

Still, that he would be in the city, within a few minutes of her, and she wouldn't know where he was, left her feeling weak-kneed.

She said, "I can offer you a ride."

He grinned at her and she realized that their hands had found their way together to clasp across the bed.

"Thanks, but no."

"You have your car somewhere?"

"Do you really want to know that?"

She dropped her chin to her chest and slowly slid her hand free, then pulled her hair back to fasten it with a band. "No."

"I didn't think so."

Neither of them said anything for a long heartbeat of time, nothing but the *whoosh-whoosh* of the ceiling fan breaking the sound of their breathing.

"When you're ready to turn yourself in…"

"You'll be the first one I call," he told her.

She nodded, unable to ask for more than that, which she wanted not because of the political clout that would come with such a move and not even because of what they had shared together in this very bed. But rather because she knew she'd be the only one who could keep him safe.

"If I need to get in touch with you?" she asked quietly.

He didn't answer for a long moment. Then he pulled her cell phone free from her waist holder and entered a number.

"My cell."

She smiled as she took the phone back. "Wouldn't Chevalier be interested in knowing I have you on speed dial?"

"Chevalier?"

She nodded as she put the cell back in her holder. "The NOPD detective working the case."

"I'm familiar with the name."

"You two have run into each other before?"

Claude shook his head. "No. Not that I know of. But I have a feeling our paths will cross before this is over and done."

"I have a feeling you're right."

Akela made out the sound of an airboat motor nearby. She told herself she should hurry out to meet her ride, to protect Claude, but since he wasn't making any moves, she wasn't in any hurry, either.

Instead she reached out for his hand again and squeezed it, searching for something more to say. "Let me know if you come across anything."

Even as she said the words, Akela couldn't help thinking they were empty ones. Unless someone stepped forward and confessed to the murder, there was probably very little to uncover that could clear Claude's name.

The reality of the situation made her throat tighten.

But she couldn't, wouldn't think of that now. Now she needed to meet her ride and pretend all was right with her world, despite that Claude Lafitte had turned it upside down.

"Go, *chere,*" he said, bringing her palm to his mouth and kissing her there, then on the inside of her wrist.

Akela was filled with the desire to kiss his mouth, but realized the sound of the boat was getting closer.

She got up and hurried out of the cabin without looking back, her secret hope being that when she saw the room again, she would be doing so as a guest and without the cloud currently hovering over Claude Lafitte's handsome head.

10

IN SOME RESPECTS, Quarter residents weren't all that unlike bayou natives in that they didn't turn in one of their own. Oh, everyone knew who he was, no matter his attempts at disguise or to blend into the background. He'd spent too much time there to expect otherwise. But no one went out of their way to point that out. They seemed to feel that whatever was going on was his business and so long as he didn't cause them any trouble, he was free to move about at will.

Claude had counted on this when he'd returned to the city the night before, after Akela had left him at the cabin. And it had served him well so far. He'd checked into a small hotel he hadn't frequented before on the outskirts of the Quarter, requesting a room near the back of the place with a quick escape route, parking a car he'd borrowed from a bayou friend nearby.

Now he stood in the darkened doorway of a bar,

staring at the entryway to Hotel Josephine across the street and up a couple of hundred feet. While he'd had luck in keeping to the shadows, he'd had no luck in figuring out a way to clear himself beyond trying to find the real killer himself. He'd carefully chosen those he'd questioned. Perhaps a little too carefully, because no one claimed to have seen her before the night he'd met her.

Could she have been a socialite slumming it? A good girl on the prowl for a bad boy for a few hours?

She wasn't from the area, of that much he was sure. Otherwise all he'd learned was that she'd been with a couple of girlfriends at the club where they'd met, who had taken off with their own companions for the night before Claude had sat next to her.

His cell phone vibrated in his back pocket. He pulled it out, frowned, then greeted his brother.

"Thierry," he said quietly.

"Where are you?"

Lately this was how their conversations had progressed—or, more accurately, regressed. They seemed to have traveled back in time to a place where Claude had constantly been getting into trouble and Thierry had been not just his brother, but his protector. He had been a teen and their mother had died of cancer, with neither of her sons having been aware of her condition.

The news had devastated Claude, while his older brother rolled more easily with the punches.

"Nearby," he said.

"So you're not in the bayou anymore."

More of a statement than a question.

"You're more at risk in the city."

"So I am."

"You don't seem very concerned."

"Because circumstances would dictate that I don't have anything to fear."

"Come on, Jean-Claude, innocent men are executed every day. You know that."

"Yes, well, I don't plan on being one of them." He moved the phone to his other ear, watching as a couple paused outside the quiet doors to the Hotel Josephine, then continued on, tourists indulging in gossip rather than lovers looking for a room. "Have you spoken to that lawyer, John Reginald?"

"Yes," Thierry said. "It appears he's not making any better progress than you are."

Not that Claude had expected him to. For all intents and purposes the NOPD had their man. Him. And they were quickly building a case around that one scenario alone.

"What do you plan to do now?"

"How about dinner at your place?"

Silence.

He paced a short distance away from the doorway. "Whatever I can."

"Have you given any thought to what's going to happen to the deal?"

The deal. His bid to buy his brother's half of Lafitte's Louisiana Boats and Tours.

"No. But I take it you have."

"Look, I think you should consider letting me sell it outright."

Claude felt as though he'd been stabbed in the back again. But this time by his own blood.

"We'll talk about this later." When he had regained control over his life.

Thierry's heavy sigh filled his ear. "Yes, well, just be careful, ya hear? And for God's sake, don't go getting yourself into any more trouble than you already have."

"Hard to imagine, that," he said, then rang off.

He stood holding his telephone for a long time. Everything was on the line with this. Everything depended on him clearing his name. His freedom. His livelihood. He couldn't imagine selling a business he'd helped build from scratch to an outsider. He'd put too much into it.

Not much had been happening at the Hotel Josephine since he'd been watching it. He supposed part of the reason might have to do with someone having been murdered there, but he was pretty sure that Josie usually did more business than he was seeing now. While potential customers seemed to linger outside, they didn't go in. In fact, in the hour that he'd been standing there he had yet to see anyone resembling a paying customer go in or out of the place.

Which wasn't helping him at all.

An NOPD squad car cruised slowly by. Claude backed farther into the shadows, watching as the driver appeared to stare straight at him, then continued on down the road. He had his hair pulled back and a leather cowboy hat low on his forehead, dark sunglasses blocking his eyes, a black leather vest and bolo over a Western shirt rounding out the look of a mysterious Southern gentleman out for a good time.

He'd never carried a gun. Oh, sure, he owned three or four, but aside from an antique Derringer he kept in a case over his desk at his office, the others were stored at his cabin at Barataria Bayou. He'd never really had much use for them outside target practice. And he didn't think it a good idea to take up the hobby of packing heat now. It would only get him into more of that trouble his brother mentioned, namely because the men he had to fear held guns of their own. And the last thing he wanted was to end up in a shooting match.

An image of Akela in her unfastened bulletproof vest checking her firearm came to mind.

As a rule, he preferred his women feminine, probably because his mother hadn't been. She'd been a combination of Ma Kettle and Annie Oakley, chewing on chaw and spitting. He'd asked her once when he'd been ten why she didn't work on her appearance more. She'd stared at him as if watching a few of his marbles roll free.

"You really think the way a woman looks matters in the scheme of things, child?" she'd asked him. Then wearing that expression that told him he still had a lot to learn in life, she'd shaken her head and walked away, leaving his question right where it was without an answer.

Akela Brooks was as far away from overtly feminine than any female he'd met in a long, long time. Yet somehow she was the most feminine woman he'd ever lain with.

Claude crossed his arms over his chest, wondering if that even made sense.

But the fact remained that up until now, up until her, he'd been drawn to women who wouldn't dream of being seen without their makeup on. To whom sexy lingerie was a calling, not just a wardrobe choice. Women who smelled of costly perfume and powders, not a simple citrus lotion. And definitely none of the women he'd dated before would want to hold a gun, much less know how to use one.

Akela…well, Akela was presentable, but she didn't do anything more than the bare minimum to make herself attractive.

Yet he couldn't seem to stop thinking about her. About how her mouth bowed open when he filled her. About how her fingers dug into the base of his back, clutching him close as she ground against him. About how the more he had of her, the more he wanted.

Of course, no good could come out of their rendezvous beyond momentary sexual satisfaction. What made it strange was that he wanted more beyond that.

The longest relationship he'd been in up to that point had been in his early twenties and had lasted six months. But sex hadn't been involved in that one. He'd gone through a period when he'd thought he might like to get married. Thierry had been engaged the first time and made the option look not only palatable but perhaps preferable.

"Just think, li'l bro," Thier had said. "You come

home to find a beautiful woman waiting for you every night."

Then his brother's engagement had ended and he'd made the mistake of having sex with his own object of affection, finding her as warm as a northerly wind in December.

He'd never given marriage another thought, even when his brother had finally found the right woman and settled down two years ago.

Claude had settled on seducing every member of the bridal party, married or otherwise.

Yet he wanted to see Akela again.

He scratched his chin and grinned. Of course, some of that fascination might have a lot to do with much of his own future being in her hands. But not even he could delude himself into thinking that was all there was at work here.

He pushed from the door and strode in the opposite direction, away from the hotel, although he couldn't be sure where he was going. But anywhere away from his current thoughts would do for the time being.

AKELA CLIMBED from her plain FBI sedan, scanning the familiar area of the Quarter around the hotel with careful deliberation. Claude was here somewhere. She could feel it. Oh, probably not within the immediate area. But he was in the Quarter, probably trying to prove the innocence he proclaimed.

It was an innocence she was becoming far too invested in making everyone else see as the truth.

She checked her firearm, closed the car door, then stepped down the walk toward Hotel Josephine. She wasn't used to being this emotionally involved in a case. Or perhaps involved wasn't the right word—unless it came to her professional standing. In that regard, she supposed she was irrevocably tied to the outcome of Claude Lafitte's case, if only because she'd been taken hostage by him and his arrest would look good in her file.

But her connection to Claude Lafitte went far beyond that now, didn't it? Not that she kidded herself into thinking that they had any sort of relationship in the traditional sense. On a normal day, during the course of a normal relationship, there would be dates and phone calls and perhaps even flowers. There had been none of that where she and Claude were concerned. Rather what did exist between them was some sort of sexual vacuum that cut her completely off from everything with which she was familiar.

Their time together on the bayou seemed as surreal as a dream. And the person she'd been there was just as unreal.

NO POSTAGE
NECESSARY
IF MAILED
IN THE
UNITED STATES

BUSINESS REPLY MAIL

FIRST-CLASS MAIL   PERMIT NO. 717-003   BUFFALO, NY

POSTAGE WILL BE PAID BY ADDRESSEE

HARLEQUIN READER SERVICE
3010 WALDEN AVE
PO BOX 1867
BUFFALO NY 14240-9952

Get FREE BOOKS and a FREE GIFT when you play the...

LAS VEGAS 7 GAME

7 7

Just scratch off the gold box with a coin. Then check below to see the gifts you get!

YES! I have scratched off the gold box. Please send me my **2 FREE BOOKS** and **gift for which I qualify.** I understand that I am under no obligation to purchase any books as explained on the back of this card.

351 HDL D7XN   151 HDL D7YP

FIRST NAME

LAST NAME

ADDRESS

APT.#	CITY

STATE/PROV.	ZIP/POSTAL CODE

(H-B-10/05)

7	7	7	Worth TWO FREE BOOKS plus a BONUS Mystery Gift!
🍒	🍒	🍒	Worth TWO FREE BOOKS!
🔔	🔔	♣	TRY AGAIN!

www.eHarlequin.com

Right now none of that mattered, though. She had a job to do, and she was going to do it. Namely, she was going to continue looking for Claude as if she hadn't spent a blissful hour with him in his bed the previous day. And if she just so happened to come across evidence that might help in his case then that would be an extra.

With the double doors to the hotel open, she stepped inside the empty lobby, immediately noticing how quiet it was—not that it had been a bustling spot before, but now there was no sound at all. No ringing telephones, no customers coming and going. Nothing.

She headed to the counter, looking for the pretty woman of mixed heritage she'd met the other day: Josie Villefranche. She was nowhere in sight. She stared down at the guest book, noticing that for the past two days the register was empty but for one random entry the day before. More than likely a tourist who hadn't known that one Miss Claire Laraway had been murdered in Room 2D.

"Can I help you, Agent Brooks?"

Akela looked up to find Josie coming in from the back, probably the kitchen area. She wiped her slender, slightly tanned hands on an apron, then ran the back of her wrist across her damp brow.

"Looks like business isn't going very well."

Josie frowned and kept her wary gaze on her. "Tends to happen when there's been a murder in the place."

"Sounds like you're familiar with the experience."

Josie shrugged and closed the guest book with a dull thud. "Let's just say that this place has seen its share of tragedies over the years."

"Josie Villefranche…are you related to the original owner, Josephine Villefranche?"

"Her granddaughter."

"I see." Josephine Villefranche, it was rumored, had been one of the Quarter's most successful madams at a time when that was saying something. She'd had the most beautiful girls and the most elite clientele.

And, if Akela wasn't mistaken, she had also experienced something along the lines of what her granddaughter was going through now when one of those girls was murdered by a member of that elite clientele.

Akela asked, "You alone here?"

"Yes."

"Aren't you afraid of being alone here?"

"No."

That intrigued Akela.

"I'm capable of protecting myself." Josie pulled a sawed-off shotgun from behind the counter.

Akela considered the firearm, picking it up and cocking it with one arm before handing it back.

"That's an illegally altered gun you've got there, Miss Villefranche."

"So sue me."

That got a smile from Akela that Josie returned.

"Do you think that Lafitte committed the murder?" Akela asked point-blank.

"Everyone's capable of just about anything. That would be my experience."

Cagey woman, this Josie Villefranche.

"But if you were the arresting officer…"

"I'm not."

"If you were…"

"If I were, I'd be looking in a couple of other directions."

"Such as?"

Josie shrugged, leading Akela to believe that she knew more than she was sharing—which didn't make much sense. Josie had been questioned at length about the circumstances surrounding the murder. But had she revealed all pertinent information?

She took out her notepad and thumbed through notes she'd taken from Chevalier.

"You were familiar with Lafitte, am I right?"

Josie sighed. "Look, I've already told the cops everything."

"Cops hoping to convict him of the crime."

"You're not?"

Now there was a question. "Let's just say I'm trying to keep an open mind about that morning's events." She turned a couple more pages. "Was there any one person Mr. Lafitte used to bring here more frequently than others?"

When Josie didn't answer right away, she knew there was.

"Who is it, Josie?"

"Look, I don't want to be getting Claude into any more trouble than he's already in."

The hotel owner knew something that would hurt, not help Claude's case. "What's her name?"

Josie stared at her for a long moment then closed her eyes. "Mimi Culpepper."

Akela wrote down the name.

"She stripped up at Chantal's for a while, but I don't think she's doing that anymore, at least not for Chantal."

"Do you know where I might find her now?"

"I've already given you more than I probably should have."

Akela didn't move.

"Ask Chantal. She'll probably know."

"And what do you know?"

"Nothing but gossip."

Gossip was never good.

Josie asked, "Look, if he's innocent, you'll help prove that, won't you?"

Akela had the feeling that Josie was asking for personal reasons.

"Yes," she said. "Yes, I will."

"Good. Then you'll want to watch what comes out of Mimi's mouth, then. She's a mean one."

Akela nodded, closed her pad, then stepped from the cramped hotel, feeling as if someone was sitting on her chest.

She really hadn't expected any results when she'd decided to stop by the hotel earlier. But if she'd dared to hope, it would have been for evidence that would help prove Claude's innocence, not his guilt.

She glanced both ways down the street then followed Josie's directions to Chantal's.

11

"YOUR DNA WAS ALL OVER the victim's body."

Claude frowned into his cell phone, not liking the sound of his attorney's voice. "Of course it was. She and I had just spent the evening having sex. If my DNA wasn't on her person, I'd be suspicious."

"What I'm trying to tell you is that there was no trace evidence of foreign DNA."

"Foreign as in from a source other than myself," Claude clarified, more for himself than Reginald. Foreign as in the real killer.

"Correct."

"You received my fax?"

His attorney sighed. "Yes, I received your fax. Unfortunately, your list of those you'd been in contact with that morning—from the baker to the dancers—doesn't help us at all. Not with the estimated time of death as imprecise as it is. You could easily have committed the murder before you left."

"Except that I didn't kill her."

Silence.

Claude tipped back the hat he was wearing. Every corner he turned he seemed to hit a dead end.

"Has anyone been over to talk to her roommate?"

He had learned that Claire Laraway had roomed with someone in an apartment over on Canal.

"I have one of the firm investigators on it now," the attorney said.

"Maybe I should—"

"Maybe you should stay as far away from the person as possible. Have you gotten a look at to-day's papers?"

Claude had a handful of the newspapers in question laid across the outside café table in front of him. If he hadn't made the front page, he was on the second page, photos of him obtained through public domain. The one he was looking at pictured him and Thierry at his brother's wedding. His brother had been cut out and what looked like a high school photograph of Claire was superimposed where Thierry's had been so it looked as if Claude was sneering at the teenager.

Not only was he a murderer, if you believed the papers, he was a child killer.

"Do me a favor and lie low," his attorney said, "unless you're ready to turn yourself over to the authorities."

Claude's fingers tightened on the small cell phone. "I didn't think so."

Claude rang off shortly thereafter and absently scanned the news piece. Strange how they could slant any story to get the response they were looking for. He supposed the idea of a murderous Don Juan wandering the streets of the Quarter sold far more newspapers than the idea that someone had set him up.

His mind caught and held on the thought. Set him up. He hadn't stopped to consider the situation from that angle before.

He asked the waiter for a pen, then used the margin of the top paper to make a list of people who might have it in for him. He stopped a few minutes later, then began drawing lines through those same names. While he had made his share of enemies over the years, he didn't think he'd pissed any of them off enough that they would want to try to set him up for murder.

And that led him back to where he'd been before: Claire Laraway had been the target all along, not him.

He bunched the papers up, then threw them away in a trash bin. He didn't care what his attorney said. He couldn't sit there and wait around until the police caught up with him.

"SOME PEOPLE you can't help protect, not if the one you're protecting them from is themselves," Chantal Gerard said.

The dim interior of the dancers' club down the street from the hotel wasn't that unlike the interior of dozens of other strip joints just like it, the difference being that this one was run by a woman, a former dancer herself, and that she was highly thought of, from what Akela could gather. Her dancers tended to stay there longer than anywhere else, and a high percentage of them actually moved on to better jobs, graduating from college and pursuing higher education. The instant she'd sought out the woman of note, she'd noticed the employees gather closer, as if prepared to protect their mother hen.

They had no cause for worry. Akela meant Chantal no harm.

"I'm not sure I'm following you," she said, squinting at the other woman across the small, round table between them. In the background, the dull *thump-thump* of bass-heavy music sounded, and on a stage nearby, a woman half danced, half tried to follow their conversation.

"What's to follow? Mimi came here looking for a job, wearing sunglasses to try to cover the black eye she'd gotten from her boyfriend. I gave her a job, but I couldn't give her any pride."

Back in the day, Chantal had probably been a looker. Blond, pretty and well-endowed, she still did justice to her tight, pink suit with sequined lapels. But time and probably atmosphere had taken their toll. Her skin hung a little slack. Her brown eyes weren't bright. And her rumbling cough spoke of a long smoking habit.

"Mimi set her sights on Jean-Claude the moment she saw him in the audience her first night."

"But you said she was involved with someone."

"Mmm. I would have liked to believe otherwise, but then her boyfriend came in and watched her like a hawk from the corner. Bad for business, that one."

"And did Claude become involved with Mimi Culpepper?"

Chantal smiled at her in a way Akela wasn't sure she liked. "About as much as Jean-Claude becomes involved with any of the girls."

Akela had to imagine she was included in that wide sweep, and that her involvement with Claude was just as meaningful.

"Of course, it didn't stop him from throwing out Mimi's boyfriend when he tried to pull her by her hair from the stage one night."

"Because they were dating?"

"Because the boyfriend was doing wrong."

"A rebel with a cause."

"Jean-Claude has always protected my girls. He has a great respect for women."

Or great appetite, whichever worked.

"Do you think he did it?" another woman, wearing a tiny silky skirt and what was akin to a bikini top, asked from where she'd just served a customer a beer.

"Of course he didn't do it," Chantal said quickly.

"How can you be so sure?" Akela asked.

"Oh, don't get me wrong. All men have it in them, you know, violence. But I don't think Jean-Claude would be stupid enough to get caught doing it."

Akela shivered, not sure she liked the answer and what it conveyed.

"Do you have a forwarding address for Mimi?"

Chantal sent the waitress to the back room. Moments later, she came out with a Rolodex card. "I always try to keep track of my dancers."

Akela gave an inquiring look.

"In case they need help."

A dancer-slash-strip-club-owner with a heart of gold.

Akela copied the information down from the card then handed it back to Chantal, thanking her for the contact and for her help.

"You know, we have amateur night here every Wednesday," Chantal said, giving her open consideration. "The guys like fresh blood, you know, if you ever feel the desire."

Akela stared at her. "Thanks, but no. There are others who need the help more than I do."

"Oh, sometimes people don't realize the kind of help they need, Agent Brooks."

She wasn't all that sure she wanted to know what the club owner meant by that as she gave the older dancer a business card and asked her to contact her should she remember something that might help in Lafitte's case.

"You don't think he did it, do you?"

Akela squinted at her through a cloud of cigarette smoke. "Pardon me?"

"Jean-Claude. You know he didn't do it."

"Just checking all angles," she said.

Chantal gave her that knowing smile again. "Mmm. Just make sure you keep your wits about you, girl."

Akela wasn't sure she liked the cryptic reference. Was Chantal implying she was at risk? Or was there a deeper, more disturbing meaning to her warning?

She navigated the web of tables and customers, making her way toward the door that stood as a beacon of light at the end of the tunnel-like joint.

She was blinking to adjust her eyesight when a figure stepped into view.

"Imagine running into you here, Brooks."

Akela closed her notepad and stared at where Detective Alan Chevalier was looking at her closely.

"Detective."

She moved to pass him.

"You know, if you come across anything that might be of interest in the Lafitte case you're to report it to me."

She thought about what both Josie and Chantal had said about Mimi Culpepper and the fact that she might hurt rather than help Claude's case and decided to keep the information to herself.

Instead, she said, "You're the first person on my list."

She understood that the way things stood, she and Chevalier were now officially on different sides of the same case. Where she was now determined to prove Claude's innocence, he was growing more determined to pound the final nail in his coffin.

She walked down the street, not looking back until she was sure Chevalier had gone into the strip joint.

She took out her cell phone and did some checking around on Mimi Culpepper. Still at the same address, utility records showed.

She climbed into her car, thinking she really should make another stop first.

CLAUDE WAS PACING his brother's office, not sure he was liking the way Thierry was talking down to him. In fact, he was positive he couldn't stand it.

"Goddamn it, Jean-Claude, what is it going to take for you to straighten up and fly right?"

Claude stopped in front of his desk. "I wasn't aware I was flying wrong."

"You've been accused of murder."

"Wrongly."

"So you're saying all this is simply a matter of being at the wrong place at the wrong time?"

"That's exactly what I'm saying."

"Story of your life, isn't it, li'l bro?"

Claude didn't know which pissed him off more: the way Thierry was looking at him with barely veiled contempt, or the way he seemed to indicate that everything Claude touched was quickly tarnished.

In that one moment it was hard to believe that at one time they'd been close, that the two brothers had been inseparably joined by blood and by creed. Then Thierry had gone to work for Brigette's family, then had married into it, and everything had changed. Suddenly the world his brother had once lived in was no longer good enough, and that went for everything in that world, including his younger brother.

"I didn't do it."

"What does it matter? So long as the police say you did it, you did it in the court of public opinion."

Claude felt as though he'd just taken one to the jaw. "There was a time not so long ago when my word would have made a world of difference to you."

Thierry had at least the good sense to look abashed. "Yes, well, that time has long passed."

"What is it that you dislike about me so, brother?" he asked. "That I refused your help? That it was important for me to make it on my own without your financial assistance?"

Thierry turned away, shoving his hands deep into his pants pocket.

"Or does one woman hold that much sway over one man."

His brother narrowed familiar eyes on him. Eyes that Claude saw in the mirror every morning.

The Lafitte brothers had a lot in common physically. Oh, Thierry might be a couple of inches taller than him, while he was by far the more physical, but the color of their dark blond hair and green eyes was the same, their unusual features made slightly different by their chosen hairstyles,

Claude's longer, Thier's shorter, neater. Their demeanors and choice of clothing were what distinguished them most, though. Even when at the office, Claude preferred jeans and T-shirts, while his brother, no matter what was on tap for the day, preferred designer suits, striped shirts and ties and shiny shoes.

Despite that they shared so much physically, Claude found he didn't recognize the expression on his brother's face anymore.

"You know, Thier, I'm half-surprised you didn't call the police the minute you realized it was me outside your office door."

His brother scratched the back of his neck, the motion more telling than either one of them wanted to admit. Once he'd become a murder suspect, it was all right if contact was kept through the telephone. But the instant Claude showed up in person, it was as if he was threatening a way of life his brother cherished more than anything.

"I won't have you tainting my life with your problems," he said, proving Claude's theory.

"Life? What are you talking about? Your public life? The man you're trying hard to build up as some sort of saint in the Garden community?" He snorted. "That's not a life—that's an illusion."

"It's a far sight better than what you've got going on."

Claude leaned his hands on his brother's polished desk. "Do you think if this had happened to you, that things would have gone down any differently? Do you believe for even an instant that you wouldn't now be in the same sinking boat I'm in?"

Thierry shook his finger at him. "Don't even try to paint me with the same brush."

"You didn't answer my question."

"Because it's too ridiculous to contemplate—I would never be in your situation."

"Why? Because you're choosier about whom you bed and where you bed them?"

He was unprepared for the fist his older brother sent flying in his direction. He managed to move out of the way at the last moment, but felt Thierry's knuckles nick his chin nonetheless.

The buzzer on the desk sounded like a much-needed reminder of where they were. Namely, they were on the tenth floor of one of the city's newer business buildings overlooking the Mississippi River, home base for Southern Cross, Inc., his brother's wife's family's company.

"Mr. Lafitte, there's an Agent Brooks here to see you."

Akela.

Claude felt an immediate desire to prevent her from hearing whatever it was his brother might have to say about him, especially considering Thier had just tried to clock him.

His brother walked him to a secondary door that would lead him around the back way, well away from the lobby where Akela would be waiting.

"Just remember, I won't have you messing up my life with your problems, Jean-Claude." He practically shoved him through the door.

"Trust me, brother, messing up your life is not what I intend. I'm merely trying to save mine."

12

AKELA'S FEET ACHED. Considering that she'd been on them more than off them all day, that wasn't a surprise. She absently rubbed the arch of her right foot under the kitchen table at her parents' house in the upscale twelve-block Garden District, close to the French Quarter yet worlds away. She sipped her herbal tea, the contents of the growing file in front of her beginning to blur.

It was nearly eight o'clock and the big house was starting its slow wind down. Akela could tell exactly what time it was by the sounds that she heard. By the voice on the news channel that came from her father's library down the hall. By the maid, Gisella, moving around her quarters on the other side of the kitchen. By the running water upstairs as her mother began her nightly beauty regimen.

Well, usually her mother would have begun her hour-long regular routine. But Akela's return a month ago had upset the delicate balance of the household. Rather than smearing cold cream on her face, her mother, Patsy Brooks, was now reading to Akela's four-year-old daughter, Daisy, in the double canopy bed Patsy had had delivered the instant she'd learned her only daughter was finally coming home.

Daisy…

It was still sometimes hard to believe that she had a child, much less a four-year-old daughter who was so much sunshine and light to her seriousness and shadows. Up until her return to New Orleans, she'd employed a live-in nanny to help with the responsibilities of a single-parent household. She knew lots of professional women who did the same. But she'd been struck to the core when she'd returned home late one night to find her own daughter throwing her skinny little arms around the college student and saying she wished she were her real mommy.

There had been something inherently wrong with the scene. And it wasn't something Akela had planned for when she'd gotten pregnant, then married fellow agent Dan McGuire. They'd divorced shortly after Daisy was born because they'd found out that not only did they not share much as a couple, but as parents their philosophies couldn't be reconciled. Simply, Dan had believed all responsibility for raising their child—outside a daily five-minute play session—rested solely on her shoulders. It hadn't taken long before Akela had begun to wonder why she needed him around at all, especially because of the extra work he created with his laundry and the dinner he insisted should be waiting for him no matter how late he got in.

Of course, by returning to New Orleans and the home she'd grown up in, Akela sometimes pondered if she'd traded a teenage nanny for her own mother. But ever since moving back into the house, Patsy had demonstrated a need to bond with a granddaughter whom she'd seen only twice a year at holidays. So Akela had taken a step back and given her the space she'd believed her mother needed.

But she was beginning to wonder if the time had come for her to reinstate herself as the primary caretaker in her daughter's young life. Truth was, even though she was under the same roof with her daughter, she missed her.

She closed the file, emptied her cup in the sink and put it into the dishwasher, then climbed the back stairs to the bedroom at the far end of the hall, a room connected to hers that had once been the green guest room.

The house she'd grown up in was mammoth by anyone's standards. With seven bedrooms, each having its own connecting bath, the hundred-year-old residence was large enough to host much of New Orleans' upper-class society. Although aside from the rare Christmas party, the house had always held only her parents, her, and the maid, though now her daughter, too.

Only as an adult did Akela find all the space a waste somehow, more suitable to a large family with lots of kids than an aging couple, their single daughter and granddaughter. Growing up, she hadn't known better, had never lived anywhere else, so had never had cause to question having so many rooms no one used. But now…

"Grammy, do you think there's such a thing as good ghosts and bad ghosts?"

Akela paused outside the doorway to her daughter's bedroom, the four-year-old's growing vocabulary never failing to amaze her.

"No, sweetling, I don't. I think there are only good ghosts."

"But if there are good ghosts, then there have to be bad ghosts, don't there? Or else how would we know the difference between the two of them?"

Akela smiled and knocked briefly on the jamb before entering the large, well-appointed room, a room befitting a princess with everything pink and white and frilly. And if ever there were a little girl who fit that description, it was her blond-haired little cherub.

"Mommy!"

The four-year-old launched herself at Akela, who now stood near the end of the bed. She easily caught her and crowded her to her chest. She noticed her mother's frown of disapproval, but Akela was thankful she didn't comment on the exuberant display of affection that she, herself, had gone without while growing up.

"Hey, sweet pea," she said, kissing the side of her daughter's fragrant hair and hugging her tightly. So small. So perfect. It was sometimes difficult to believe that she'd made this delightful creature. "Are you enjoying story time?"

"Oh, yes," Daisy said. "Very much so."

Akela drew back and looked into her round, soft face. "I was thinking that maybe tomorrow night Mommy could read to you. What do you think of that?"

The delight on her daughter's face was diluted by the disappointment on her mother's. Akela ignored it and concentrated on the little girl in her arms instead.

"I'd like that very much."

"Good." She rounded the bed. "So are you all set? Teeth all brushed? Face washed?"

"All ready," Daisy said, scrambling under the covers Akela held for her then tucked in around her slender body.

"Grandma, would you like to say good-night first?" Akela asked pointedly.

She didn't miss the flash of irritation on her mother's face.

"Good night, Daisy Mae." She kissed her grand-daughter's cheek and gave the covers a final pat.

"Good night, Grammy."

"Grandmother," her mother corrected.

"Yes, right. Good night, Grandmother."

Akela bit her bottom lip, wondering if her mother just couldn't help herself. The constant corrections, the grooming, the teaching. Of course, all the lessons had obviously been lost on Akela. While she could outmanner most, she found she no longer wanted to. There was something…cold about holding one's head just so and acting the paragon of discretion over all else, especially over honest emotion.

She waited until Patsy had left the room then sat down on her daughter's bed.

"Are you happy here, baby?" Akela asked, tucking Daisy's almost white hair behind her tiny shell ears.

"Oh, yes, Mommy. Very much so."

The phrase was a new and often used one and never failed to make Akela smile.

"I hear you're doing very well at day school."

Daisy nodded. "I like it."

"And they apparently like you." She tickled her plump belly, taking great joy in her daughter's peal of laughter.

Sometimes Akela wondered how it was she'd gotten to be so lucky. While some might judge her situation with the detachment of an outsider, call her to task for divorcing a man who hadn't really done anything wrong, or for having a child at all given her chosen vocation, she couldn't imagine her life without the four-year-old in it. Without her wide, baby-toothed grin. Her constant questions. Her ceaseless enthusiasm. Not a day went by that she didn't grow in some way, be it physically, emotionally or intellectually. And Akela reveled in every subtle and obvious step, wanting to hold on to the youngster tightly with both hands even as she prepared to loosen that same grip so she could grow into a balanced and independent young woman.

Of course, that Daisy was the complete opposite of her was the source of some confusion. She responded well to her grandmother's lessons, seeming, in fact, to blossom under Patsy's attention, while Akela remembered being in constant eye-roll mode.

She picked up a framed photo of Daisy from the nightstand and stared at it. Only closer inspection showed it wasn't her daughter at all, but herself at around the same age.

Had she really been all that different from the little girl now watching her curiously from the bed?

She put the frame back down. "Sleep tight, munchkin," she said, kissing Daisy soundly. "And don't let those bedbugs bite."

"See you in the morning light," the four-year-old said with an exaggerated yawn.

Akela slowly left the room, switching off the lamps but leaving the door open a crack so the hall light could break the darkness. The one thing she remembered as a child was the darkness.

"You indulge her too much," her mother said when she'd reached the stairs.

"And you're too stern with her."

Even as Akela said the words, she knew they weren't fair. They were said in a knee-jerk reaction to her mother's criticism, a childish one she was beginning to doubt she'd ever truly grow out of.

"Look, Akela, I don't wish to argue with you."

"Good, because I don't want to argue with you, either, Mother."

She began to go back downstairs, then paused midway down. "Just so you know, now that we're settled and Daisy has gotten used to you and Dad, I'm going to be taking a more active role in my daughter's life."

"As well you should."

"Which means you're going to have to take a less active one."

Her mother fell silent.

She didn't mean to hurt her mother—really, she didn't. But if this arrangement was going to work, she would need the room to redefine her relationship with her young daughter, and that included the retreat of her own parents.

Patsy nodded. "Very well, then."

CLAUDE LAY BACK on the bed in the seedy hotel room, the ceiling fan doing little but churning the hot air and pushing it back at him. He was alone— no willing female at his side—not for lack of opportunity, but for lack of interest, more specifically his interest. A first for him, in a string of firsts he'd been encountering lately. Women had always been a source of escape for him, although he really hadn't understood the meaning of that word until now. Because despite everything hanging over his head, he couldn't seem to escape one woman: Akela Brooks.

He picked up the wind-up brass alarm clock from the bed stand and stared at it in the dim light shining in from Bourbon Street. After midnight. He put the clock back down, listening to the dueling sounds coming from two different jazz bands from two different bars and the people talking as they passed the open windows. It wasn't all that long ago that he'd been one of those people. Out for the night to see what it had to offer. Maybe finding a companion and going with her to a room not unlike the one he was in now.

But the only woman he wanted was the one he couldn't have.

He dry washed his face and shut off the television in the corner, then tossed the remote to the foot of the bed. Sleep was pretty much out for him. The more he seemed to dig for information on Claire, the deeper he seemed to be implicated in her murder. Hell, if he didn't know better, he might begin to think he *had* murdered her.

He reached for his cell phone, pressing the keypad so the display lit up. Then he dialed the last number he should be dialing if he knew what was good for him.

AKELA REREAD the passage in the original police report one of Chevalier's men had taken, unable to concentrate on the words or their meaning. She shifted on the two pillows she'd positioned behind her back and glanced toward the closed window and the lace sheers preventing her from seeing more than the glow of the moon just beyond. She sighed and put the papers down on the table before flicking out the light and focusing across the room at nothing outside, and everything inside herself, longing for an unnamable something. Fresh air, perhaps, instead of the conditioned air that filled the house. The scent of things growing, rather than the freshener that always made the place smell like roses.

Claude.

She hadn't been able to get her mind off Claude since coming up to her room a couple of hours earlier. She kept wondering where he was. Whether he was alone. And if he wasn't, then whom he had chosen to spend the night with.

She caught herself rubbing her arms and stopped.

She wasn't used to this feeling. This obsessing over someone, especially someone who was not only a fugitive from the law but opposite to the kind of men she'd been attracted to before now. Someone who had made her come to life in a way no other man had been capable of.

She pushed from the bed and stepped toward the window, not stopping until she had the sheers pushed back and had opened the pane, breathing in deep gulps of the humid air. Rather than making her feel better, the memory of what it had been like in the bayou, rasping for breath after having sex with Claude, came rushing back.

She heard a faint electronic chirp. She turned and looked toward the side of the bed where her cell phone had lit up indicating she had an incoming call. She slowly walked to pick it up, staring at the number on the display.

Claude.

Akela clutched the phone to her chest, wondering if she dared answer.

Wondering if she dared not answer…

13

CLAUDE COULD IMAGINE Akela in a nice room somewhere across town staring at the phone and wondering whether or not to answer it. He couldn't blame her. If his head were screwed on tightly, he wouldn't have put her in the position he had. Then again, he'd had no choice in the matter. He hadn't asked her to come out to the bayou looking for him. Yes, he had asked her to stay behind, though he'd never in a million years expected her to. But she had. And from that moment on he'd had absolutely no control over what happened next.

The cell kept ringing. Surely by now she'd heard it and made her decision not to answer. He began to pull the phone away from his ear to disconnect when the line stopped ringing.

"Hello?"

The sound of her voice was like a salve to an open wound.

"Akela," he said on a breath.

He didn't apologize for calling her. And she didn't ask him to. He guessed that maybe she'd needed to hear his voice as much as he'd needed to hear hers.

He caught the sound of something on her end.

"What are you doing?" he asked.

There wasn't an immediate response. Then he heard the click of what sounded like a door opening. Or closing.

"I'm looking in on my daughter."

Claude's chest tightened.

Her daughter…

He hadn't stopped to consider that the capable, sexy agent would have a life outside her job. Hadn't guessed at her being married, or divorced. Hadn't thought of her as a mother.

That she and another man had created a child together made him hurt in a way that he hadn't known he could.

"Her name's Daisy. She's four years old."

Daisy. The whimsical name made him smile.

"She's a beautiful blonde with a smile that'll steal your heart."

He could envision Akela smoothing back the little girl's hair while she slept.

"And her father?"

"Sees her every other holiday, a couple of weeks in the summer, and calls on her birthday."

"You were married?"

"Yes."

But they weren't any longer.

The knowledge that Akela had belonged to another man, no matter for how brief a time, struck him to the bone somehow. He'd gotten the distinct impression that she had never made love to anyone as she'd made love with him. If that were the case, how could she have promised her heart to someone who didn't move her?

Claude clenched the bedsheet in his hand. Then again, wasn't it he who drew the line staunchly between love and sex? So if there could be great sex without love, didn't it stand to reason that there could also be great love without great sex?

"Penny for your thoughts," Akela said softly.

If only she knew what he was thinking. "Where are you now?"

"Back in my room."

"Alone?"

He swore he could hear her smile. "Alone."

"What are the chances of tempting you out?"

She paused, as if trying to figure out his question. "Out? As in outside the house?"

He nodded. "Yes."

"Slim to none."

Claude stretched his neck and stared at the ceiling. "Because of your daughter."

"No. My parents and the maid are here. I can't come because it wouldn't be a very good idea."

He wanted to ask good for whom. It would be very good for him—and completely selfish. Because he was looking for a way to banish the clingy shadows of the night. And for whatever reason she was the only one who could do that for him right now.

"Where are you?" she asked.

"So you can come?"

He heard her swallow. "No."

"Then it's probably not a good idea if I tell you."

"No. I don't suppose it is."

Akela stretched back across her bed, her mind telling her she should find a way to end this conversation, which shouldn't be taking place. The moment he'd said her name, he'd connected a bridge from their time outside of time in the bayou to the here and now and reality. She wasn't sure she was ready for that. Wasn't sure she was ready for what it could mean.

Still, she told herself, it wasn't as if he was physically in the room with her, no matter how much she felt that he could have been. They were talking on the phone. That was okay, wasn't it?

She wasn't sure whom she was asking that

question. All she knew was how dark the night was, how hypnotic Claude's voice.

She'd never been one for long phone conversations. Not with her friends. Not with lovers. Not with her ex-husband. Yet she found herself reluctant to end her current call with Claude.

For some reason she couldn't put her finger on, the bed linens felt softer against her skin, left partially bare by her nightgown. Her nipples felt highly sensitive and she squeezed her thighs tightly together, compensating for an absence she felt down to her toes.

"Where are your hands now?"

Akela swallowed hard. "One's gripping the phone…"

"And the other?"

"Lying on the top sheet. Why?"

"Because I'd like to borrow them for a while."

Borrow them? As in pretend they were touching him?

"Borrow them to touch you the way I wish I were touching you now."

Akela felt as if her entire body had been reawakened.

He didn't say anything for a long moment and she held her breath, wondering if he dared to continue.

His voice came back, low and provocative.

"First I want you to uncurl your fingers from the sheet."

She wondered how he knew she was doing that and slowly did as he asked, smoothing her palm against the sheet's softness.

"Now, I want you to rest it against your stomach."

"I'm lying on my stomach."

"Better."

She heard his voice catch and Akela thought of the picture she made in his mind, of her pressed against the mattress, the curve of her bottom offered up to him.

"What do you want me to do with it?"

"Hmm? Oh, your hand."

Akela smiled, surprised she had caught him off guard with such a simple statement.

"I want you to press it against your outer thigh."

She felt her skin rasp against the silky material of her nightgown as she pulled her hand close against her side and splayed her fingers against the flesh of her thigh.

"Now...slide it upward."

She closed her eyes, listening to the throb of her heartbeat, the easy, sexy cadence of his voice, then trailed her fingers upward.

"No, no...slower..."

Akela shivered as she slowed the movement of

her fingers. Up over her hip…her abdomen…the outer swell of her breast.

"What are you wearing?"

"A nightgown."

She heard his quiet chuckle. "I can't see you, Akela. You're going to have to be more descriptive than that."

"What do you see me wearing?"

"A white silky number with too much material."

Her nightgown was cream colored, but otherwise he was on the mark.

"I want you to take it off."

Akela glanced toward her bedroom door. Despite the monstrous size of the house, she'd always been aware that she wasn't alone there. She'd never given herself over to self-pleasure, even in her teenage years when the simple feel of a pillow between her legs had threatened to topple her over the edge.

"Have you done it?"

"No. Wait."

She reached down and bunched the silky material in her hand, tugging it until she finally pulled it up over her head, tousling her hair in the process.

"There."

She could have sworn she heard him groan.

"Are you still lying on your stomach?"

"Yes."

"Okay…I want you to put your hand where it was before."

She did so, noticing the heat of her own skin beneath her palm.

"Gently shift your fingers so they're cupping your breast…."

Akela spread her fingers and worked them in between her body and the mattress, caressing her own breast. She gasped when a bone-deep shudder rushed over her body.

"Is your nipple hard?"

"Uh-huh."

"I want you to focus your attention there. Bring your finger and thumb together until you're pinching the pink flesh…."

She followed his directions like a woman who had no control over her own body. And for a moment she felt like it wasn't, in fact, her own fingers plucking her puckered flesh, but Claude's.

"Harder…"

Akela pressed her face into her pillow to muffle her shallow breathing as she pinched her own nipple to the point of pain. It didn't escape her notice that it brought her exquisite pleasure.

"Don't press against the mattress."

Akela licked her lips. "What?"

"Your hips. Don't press them against the mattress."

How did he know that's what she was doing?

She stopped.

"Now, what I want you to do…"

Akela methodically, slowly, followed each of his murmured commands, moving her hand over to her other breast, pausing in between the two mounds of flesh until she thought she might cry out with the need to have him touching her the way he was having her touch herself. For long moments he left her with her fingers splayed against her stomach, feeling her own quick, shallow intakes of breath.

Then, finally, he was directing her farther south, toward the triangle of hair hungry for attention she had so far denied it.

"Are you wearing panties?"

"Hmm? Yes."

"What color?"

Akela had forgotten. She had to look down. "Black."

"Mmm. Good." Was it her or had his voice gotten softer? "For now I want you to work around those sexy panties… No, no…keep your thighs together…."

He directed her fingers up over the elastic and

against the soft cotton until she was probing her swollen flesh through the material.

"Easy…easy…"

He must have caught on to how close she was to crisis, because his command came at just the right time to keep her from toppling over the edge into searing sensation.

He asked her to move her hand back up to her stomach, where he made her pause until she got her breathing back under control.

"Are you ready?"

Akela wanted to ask what for, but couldn't seem to squeeze the words out of her throat.

He chuckled softly. "I'll take that as a yes. Now…"

At his command, she slid her fingers back toward the top elastic of her panties. But instead of bypassing the entrance, he directed her this time inside them, moving lower and lower still, until her fingers touched her springy curls.

"Spread your legs for me now, Akela. Yes, yes, that's it…."

She did as he bade, finding that even as she did so, she instinctively lifted her bottom farther up into the air as if seeking a meeting he wasn't there to give her.

"Slide your fingers into your soft folds…."

She did as he asked, her heart nearly exploding in her chest, a light sheen of sweat clinging to her skin.

"Are you wet?"

Akela moaned. "So wet…so hot."

It was a long moment before he spoke again and she was half afraid she'd lost him. Then he came back.

"Now, with your first two fingers, I want you to find your sweet bijou…."

He directed her to thrust them deep inside her dripping flesh while pressing her hips into the mattress.

Just like that, the world exploded into a cloud of red-hot sensation. She cried out into her pillow, burying her face deep in the soft material as her flesh pulsed around her own fingers.

"Thrust them again, Akela, baby…thrust them again…."

She did as he asked, surprised that the movements drew out her orgasm until she was bucking against the mattress and her own hand, wishing all the while that it was him.

Finally she collapsed, spent, against the bed, her breath coming in rapid gasps. She rolled over, her thighs spread wide, her chest heaving. She had no problem at all imagining him on the other end of the line, his hand grasping his own rigid member at the root, spilling his seed all over his muscled stomach. She wished she were there to spread the warm proof of his passion over his skin, to run her tongue over him, lick him clean.

She hadn't been aware she'd said the words aloud until she heard his very vocal groan on the other end of the line.

"Now I'm putting my mouth over the top…flicking my tongue around the head…sucking…."

Akela's own hand remained between her legs, fondling her slick flesh as she whispered to him.

Only after she was sure he had come, did she slowly remove her fingers from her panties, running her fingertips over her stomach and up to her breast.

"Claude?"

"Hmm?"

"Good night."

He chuckled quietly. "It's definitely much better after having talked to you."

She smiled and disconnected the call, holding the phone between her breasts for long, silent moments. Then, finally, she put the receiver on the nightstand and rolled over, hoping that in her dreams her own hands would be replaced by Claude's.

14

ONE OF THE ADVANTAGES of being an FBI agent was access to considerable resources. Each city and county had to account for every lab test, every autopsy, a monetary value placed on each item and coming out of a fixed budget. But with federal involvement, Akela was able to green-light direct funding of New Orleans's criminal investigation unit.

She had already been through the preliminary information Chevalier had passed on to her, but she had the feeling that she hadn't had access to everything. Wishful thinking? Maybe so. But she also knew that the jaded detective was collecting only the evidence that would place Claude behind bars for a long, long time to come. Anything else would be easily allowed to fall by the wayside because, as Chevalier had so conveniently put it, "Why cloud the issue?"

It was just past 7:00 a.m. She'd purposely got an early start that morning after putting in a phone call and finding out the NOPD head forensics expert in charge of the case liked to come into the "office" in the dead of night, when she felt her biorhythms worked more efficiently. She would be calling it a "night" at around eight or so. So if Akela wanted to talk to her, it would have to be now.

Akela flashed her ID at the security guard posted outside the crime laboratory, then pushed open the door to the examining room, struck immediately by the smell of cleaning solution and blood.

"Dr. Landau?"

The sound of metal clanking against metal then a muffled, "Back here."

Akela navigated the large room, around tables and counters and large wastebaskets in the general direction she thought she'd heard the voice. There, positioned over a body with her magnifying glass hovering over an open chest cavity, sat a woman of about her age, her brown hair pulled back and under a blue protective cap, her clothes covered by a blue smock, rubber gloves on her hands. Akela forced herself not to look directly at the body of a middle-aged man and put the tray of coffee and doughnuts she held down on a nearby table.

"Mmm, thanks," Julie Landau said without looking up at her. She blindly reached for one of the coffees, popped the lid, then took a long pull from it.

Akela looked around the quiet area, careful not to specifically acknowledge much of what she was looking at. The first time she'd had to ID a body, she'd upchucked everything on the sidewalk outside the medical examiner's office. She knew better than to challenge that gag instinct now.

Landau finally pushed the magnifying glass away, slid her own reading glasses to the top of her capped head, then looked at Akela.

"Not a lot of people know how to do that."

"Do what?"

"Keep quiet." She smiled then took off her rubber gloves one by one. "They're usually reminding me of who they are or asking questions when I'm obviously absorbed in something else."

She reached for something on a counter to her other side and handed Akela a folder.

"I think this is what you're looking for."

Akela read the file folder label marked *Laraway, Claire,* then opened it, scanning the top page as Landau swiveled around on her stool and checked out the doughnuts. She chose a sprinkle-covered one, shook it then bit into it.

"It says here you found a hair inside the neck wound?"

Landau nodded. "Yeah. Didn't belong to the victim or the suspect."

Akela stared at her. She'd been told that there had been no trace evidence from an outside source. "How can you be sure?"

The forensics expert raised a brow. "Because I identified two types of hair from the bed and the one in the wound didn't match them. And there was only one specimen."

"Which would indicate…"

"That there was a third person involved."

Akela's chest lightened as she read the rest of the material. The investigation indicated that the killer had been left-handed, given the depth and sweep of the wound. Claude was right-handed. But, of course, that bit of information meant little because he could have done it that way to throw off the investigation.

She shivered.

"Can you tell if the hair belongs to a man or a woman?"

"Not yet. I've sent it to Virginia for further analysis." She chewed on her doughnut. "I will tell you I believe the hair was planted."

"Planted?"

"Mmm." She used her pinkie to wipe a pink sprinkle from the side of her mouth. "There was something about the way it was placed, nice and neat and with the follicle attached, inside the wound that set off an alarm or two." She squinted at her. "I'm trained to pay attention to those alarms."

A planted hair indicated premeditation. Given that the entire case against Claude hinged on the murder being a crime of passion, there was no room for premeditation.

Akela smiled at the doctor.

"Looks like I gave you the info you were looking for."

"Pardon me?"

She polished off the doughnut, scrubbed up and then reached for a fresh pair of rubber gloves. "You hoping the guy didn't do it?"

Akela closed the file. "Let's just say that there are a few other things that set off an alarm or two of my own. And I'm trained to pay attention to those alarms."

CLAUDE KNEW it probably wasn't the best idea he'd had, but he'd already proven his inability to sit around and let his fate be decided for him. Hell, given that he couldn't truly trust his own brother in the situation, he had only himself to rely on.

He jimmied the lock on the door to the apartment Claire had shared with a woman named Joann Bennett, a skill he'd picked up on the street long ago. He'd watched a woman he guessed was Claire's roommate leave a few minutes ago, probably on her way to work. Since Claire's body had been flown back to her home in Toledo, Ohio, life, he guessed, had to go on as usual.

He slipped inside the small, dark apartment and stood still for a moment, allowing his eyesight to adjust. A look around showed a modest place decorated with bright colors. In the corner was a collection of boxes. Claire's things? Claude suspected they were. Probably Bennett was already in the market for a new roommate. After all, dead roommates couldn't help make the rent.

He opened the top box, peered at the various photo albums and high school yearbooks there, then moved the box aside and opened the next one. He wasn't sure what he was looking for. Something, anything to prove his innocence would do the trick. But exactly what that something would be, he didn't know.

During his questioning of those who had seen Claire with friends that night, he hadn't leaned of a boyfriend, longstanding or otherwise. Of course, he couldn't actually approach her roommate or any of her friends himself, not without fear of scaring them off, seeing as his picture was featured on the cover of the only city newspaper. So he'd taken this chance.

He heard a key in the door lock.

Damn.

He quickly put the boxes back together and ducked into one of the two bedrooms that looked as if it may have been Claire's, given the way it was cleaned up with no personal touches remaining. He closed the door partially and stood off to the side, watching as the woman who had left earlier returned, holding a drugstore bag. Apparently she hadn't gone to work.

Claude debated what he should do from there. The roommate disappeared inside the bathroom and moments later he heard running water. He stepped to the window. The apartment was on the first floor, but there were bars on the window that had been painted over.

He heard a knock on the apartment door. Looking in that direction through the window, he saw none other than Akela checking her watch.

He couldn't question the roommate, but Akela most certainly could.

AKELA FELT the unmistakable feeling that she was being watched again. It might be the middle of the morning, and broad daylight, but just being at this end of the Quarter, outside the main drag, with sparse foot and car traffic, put her on edge. She checked her firearm, then readjusted her suit jacket.

"Miss Bennett?" She addressed the young

woman who answered the door. "It's Agent Akela Brooks with the FBI. I spoke to you on the phone this morning."

"Yes. Come in."

She followed the young woman inside the small apartment. "Thanks for agreeing to see me. I understand that police have already been by and it must be difficult for you to relive the incident…."

The young woman shrugged. "Claire didn't live here all that long. Two months."

Akela took her notepad out and jotted down the information. "You weren't friends before then?"

"No. We met through an ad I put in the paper looking for someone to share the rent." She gestured toward one of two doors. "Like I'm doing again."

"You two didn't become close during those two months?"

Akela already knew that Joann Bennett hadn't been with Claire the night she met Claude. But other than that, she knew little about Claire beyond that she was a paralegal and had been checking into taking a few prelaw courses at Tulane. At twenty-seven, perhaps she'd decided that the life she'd mapped out wasn't quite panning out the way she'd hoped and she'd decided to promote herself from paralegal to lawyer.

"No, we didn't. I spend a lot of time over at my boyfriend's place."

"The two of you never went out?"

"No. I mean, maybe lunch once or twice. But while I never saw anyone, I got the impression she was involved with someone, too."

Akela noted that, then pointed toward the boxes. "Are these her things?"

"Yeah." She sighed. "I don't know what I'm going to do with them. I talked to her mother yesterday, but she didn't seem all that interested in Claire's personal belongings. Her sister is supposed to be calling me sometime today or tomorrow. I'm going to ask if she wants me to ship the things to her. I can only imagine how much it's going to cost me."

Akela stepped closer to the boxes in question. "Do you mind if I take a look?"

"Sure. Go ahead." She glanced toward the small kitchenette. "I was just going to make some tea. Would you like a cup?"

"Yes. That would be nice, thanks."

Akela opened the top box and thumbed through a photo album filled with pictures probably taken during Mardi Gras a couple of years back.

"She kept a diary," Joann said, bringing in a plate of cookies. "I think it's in the third box down."

Diary.

Akela frowned. "Did you tell the police about it?"

"Yeah. The detective, Chevalier, didn't appear all that interested, though."

Of course, Chevalier wouldn't be interested. He already had his killer—or would when he arrested Claude, anyway.

Joann went back into the kitchen as Akela moved the top two boxes out of the way. She found a leather-bound journal near the top of the third one. She opened it and read the date on the first page. A year ago. She turned away from the boxes and closer to the front window where the light was better. The entries were written in neat script, all in black ink. Seemed Claire Laraway had passed penmanship with flying colors. She leafed through the entries, paying close attention to any entries that appeared different than the others. She found one twenty pages in. The words were cramped as if written in a hurry.

> I can't believe he did this to me again. I mean, how many times is a girl supposed to be stood up before she gets the hint?

Akela read through the remainder of the entry. While it was apparent the subject was a man she'd been dating for an unspecified period of time, there was no mention of a name. Instead Claire had used words like *the jerk* to describe him.

She turned a few pages.

'C' told me he asked his wife for a divorce today.

Akela frowned at the use of an initial rather than a full name. She checked out the date noted at the top of the page. Two weeks ago.

So Claire had been dating a married man she called 'C.'

"Anything interesting?" Joann asked, bringing in two cups of hot steaming water from the kitchen along with a small box of tea selections.

"Maybe."

Akela sat down opposite her and chose a tea, putting the bag in to steep. "Have you read this?"

Joann shook her head as she selected her own tea. "No. I mean, I thought about it, but something creeped me out about the whole thing, you know, now that she's dead."

Akela nodded. "I agree."

"You probably have to do stuff like this all the time, though, don't you? I mean, go through dead people's stuff."

Akela had never really looked at her job that way. "Sometimes."

She got that feeling of being watched again and fought a shiver, even though the room was warm.

She put the journal down on the coffee table and then went about taking the bag out of her tea. "You wouldn't happen to have come across Claire's address book or anything, would you?"

Joann shook her head. "No. I think she might have had it in her purse or something. Maybe her mom got her personal stuff from the hospital or something."

"Maybe." She crossed her legs. "Did Claire happen to mention anyone, a guy whose name may have begun with a *C*?"

Joann appeared to think about it. "No. I don't think so."

"Do you have a phone here?"

"You can use my cell if you want."

"No hard line?"

"No. Both Claire and I used our cell phones, so what's the point?"

What was the point indeed? She wondered if there were any old cell phone bills in the boxes and guessed that anything that was Claire's would be in there. Joann struck her as a thorough person.

"God, what am I going to with that stuff?"

Joann said. "I have a girl coming by this afternoon to take a look at the room."

Akela blew on her tea and took a sip. "I could probably take the boxes off your hands if you want."

Joann looked at her hopefully. "Could you really? I mean, I'd have to call her mother and let her know you have them, not that I think she'd care. She said something like, 'What the hell do you want me to do with them?' when I told her about the boxes."

"No problem. I can put them in the mail after I'm done with them."

"Oh, that would be so great!"

Silence settled between them as they pretended interest in their tea.

Then Joann asked, "Is it true what they say? You know, about dead people talking?"

Akela lifted the journal. "In this case, it appears to be true. And Claire has a lot to say."

She only hoped there was something in there that would help clear Claude's name.

15

AKELA HEFTED the last of the boxes into the trunk of her plain agency sedan and thanked Joann Bennett for her help. She stood for a long moment, watching as the young woman returned to her apartment then closed the door.

In her job as agent, she'd been exposed to many interesting situations, today's circumstances ranking low on the list, but nonetheless unusual. Joann Bennett had seemed virtually unconcerned that her roommate had been murdered. Akela supposed part of her behavior might have to do with the mentality shared by many, that since it had happened to Claire, the odds of something similar happening again so close to home were slim.

Still, Akela couldn't help feeling concerned on Joann's behalf. She knew victims were chosen for their denial abilities. And Bennett was not that unlike, say, a waitress at a strip joint who decided to walk home late at night thinking she didn't have anything to worry about, not thinking about the fact that a potential rapist could be following on her heels.

She closed the trunk then let herself into the car, putting Claire's journal in the backseat. Of course, her own sense of danger came from the feeling she, herself, was being watched lately. It didn't matter what time of the day or night, there, just under her skin, was the unmistakable sense that she wasn't alone no matter where she was.

Akela checked her cell phone then started the engine.

Someone opened the passenger door.

Akela automatically reached for her firearm, then looked over.

"Claude!" She retracted her hand, but found the traitorous limb shaking. "I wouldn't do that again unless you're after a piece of lead."

He climbed inside to sit on the passenger's seat, closed the door then nodded toward the street. "It would probably be a good idea if you started driving."

She put the car into gear and headed farther out of the Quarter.

"What were you doing at Claire's apartment?" she asked.

"Waiting in the other room."

Akela looked at him sharply. "Bennett knew you were there?"

"No. She'd left and I thought she'd gone to work so I let myself in to go through the boxes you now have in your trunk."

Akela tightened her hands on the steering wheel. "Adding B and E to your list of arrest warrants isn't going to help your case any."

She concentrated on driving, but could feel his intense gaze on her profile.

"What would you have me do, Akela? Wait to see what happens first—if I get arrested or have to turn myself in?"

She suddenly had difficulty swallowing.

He had a point, of course. She couldn't see herself waiting around and putting her future blindly in the hands of others, either.

Still, she wished it hadn't been him she'd felt watching her. It made her feel uncomfortable in a way she was loath to admit.

"What did you uncover?" he asked.

She reached into the backseat and handed him the journal. "I haven't had a chance to go over the whole thing yet, but it appears the victim was involved with a married man and they were experiencing difficulties."

He accepted the journal. "Her name was Claire."

Akela was so accustomed to keeping a professional wall up between her and victims she sometimes forgot that they had names. It was called survival.

She asked, "Did Claire mention anything to you about being involved with anyone else?"

"No."

She was both disappointed and relieved that he didn't elaborate. Likely he and Claire hadn't done much talking during their time together.

"Did you see a name?" he asked.

She took the open journal from his hands. "Why? So you can break into his place?"

She put the journal in the backseat again and watched as he lifted the leather cowboy hat he wore and ran his fingers through his damp, tousled hair.

"This waiting is driving me crazy," he said, an edge to his voice she hadn't heard before.

Without knowing that's what she was going to do, Akela reached across and put her hand on top of his, slowly stroking it. "You know, there is something you can do."

"Turn myself in? Not an option. Anyway, how would that help anything?"

"Depending on how you do it, you could turn public opinion in your favor."

He didn't say anything for a long time. Akela gauged that he might be ready to hear more.

"If you proclaim your innocence and good faith by turning yourself over to authorities, stating your trust that your name will be cleared, it could make a world of difference."

It could also save his life.

At this point, with the evidence Chevalier had already compiled against him, if a takedown went wrong and Claude was...shot, his guilt would never be questioned.

He stared at her. "My name and likeness are already all over the papers, Akela. I'm being called the Quarter Killer."

That, in her opinion, was all the more reason for him to turn himself in. The court of public opinion was already in full swing, based on information she had little doubt Chevalier was leaking to the press outlining a damning case against the man next to her. And the longer he didn't respond to the charges, the worse it looked for him.

"Pull over here."

She was surprised by the request. She hadn't known what she expected once he'd climbed into her car, but it wasn't that he would leave as quickly as he'd shown up.

"Claude..." She touched his arm when he moved to get out.

He looked at her, his gaze intense, his features somber.

"Look, I'm worried about you. The longer this drags on, the worse it gets for you." She reached for her purse and took out her pad and pen, writing down a name then handing it to him. "This is one of my contacts at the *Times-Picayune*. Call her. Tell her I sent you."

"What if she calls NOPD?"

"She won't. She has too much to gain by getting an exclusive scoop from the suspect himself."

He didn't say anything.

"At least promise me you'll consider calling her. At the very least it can help create some positive groundwork."

"For when I surrender to authorities?"

Akela looked away, unable to hold his gaze.

They both knew that eventually that's what it would come down to.

He climbed out of the car, but paused before closing the door.

"I didn't know you had a daughter," he said.

His comment surprised her. Aside from being completely off topic, that he'd made a point of bringing up her personal life confused her.

"Do you have a picture?"

She wasn't sure what to make of his question, so she just opened up the glove compartment where she kept her wallet and flipped it open.

Claude took it.

"She's beautiful."

She smiled. "Yes, she is, isn't she?"

He handed back the wallet, a cryptic look on his face.

"Claude?"

He waited.

"Promise me you'll think about what I said."

He nodded, then closed the door.

Akela sat, watching as he strode down the street, then turned a corner, disappearing from sight.

LATER THAT NIGHT, Akela wasn't sure what was worse: hearing from Claude, or not hearing from him.

She lay in Daisy's double bed, the four-year-old cuddled up to her side, reading the journal she'd exchanged for the fairy tale after her daughter had fallen asleep in the middle of chapter two. She had her cell phone with her, and the house was quiet enough for her to think that her parents had long since called it a night. But rather than going to her own room, she cuddled Daisy a little closer then rubbed the creased skin between her eyes, going over the notes she'd made from the journal so far.

It was obvious that Claire had had an ongoing affair with a married man. Akela could only count four times that Claire had actually met him—at least those were the only meetings she'd taken time to write about, the journal far from a daily dairy but more a place to record happy and angry memories. Most of it focused on her job as a paralegal where she called the pay paltry and the stress high. The other, more personal entries had never mentioned the married man by name, although she'd mentioned other men's names. Akela didn't think Claire actually called him 'C' but rather guessed the generic reference was rooted in her own guilt associated with the situation.

Akela wished she had chosen a different initial. That the name Claude began with the letter she used didn't bode well, even if Claude was very much single.

It was obvious Claire had expected the man to leave his wife for her. Did any woman ever get into such a sticky situation without believing that? But as time and frustration wore on, Claire's notes became more caustic and angry, at one point even mentioning having found out where the man lived and paying a visit to his wife, to whom she also hadn't referred by name. Akela checked three times, but there was no follow-up mention of the meeting or how it had gone.

Not that it would have made a difference. If her married lover's name had been Charlie, the odds of finding him were slim to none. The young woman had been nothing if not private. A visit to her office had offered up very little additional information. She'd lunched for an hour every day, but never invited anyone to come with her, and never talked about where she'd been or whom she may have lunched with outside the office. She'd never received calls at work, but did take the occasional call on her cell phone.

Akela read a note she'd made to herself to check for cell bills in the boxes still in her trunk.

So what had happened to Claire the night she'd hooked up with Claude? Had she gone out planning to get even with a lover who would probably never leave his wife? And had that married lover then murdered her for her efforts, pinning it on Claude?

Her left arm began to feel prickly from holding it in the same position for too long. She put the journal on the nightstand then gently moved Daisy until she was lying by herself, smoothing back her hair when the four-year-old sighed and tried to snuggle again. She got up with a minimum of fuss, switched off the light, collected her things, then made her way to her room down the hall. After she'd closed her door after herself, she leaned against the solidly carved wood, immediately aware again of that sensation of being watched. She shuddered, leaving the light off as she placed the journal on a dresser then made her way to bed.

For long minutes she lay there, arms at her sides, staring at the outline of the cypress tree outside on her ceiling. She'd known Claude had been a frequent visitor to Hotel Josephine. Had anyone asked the pretty owner if Claire had been a regular customer? She couldn't remember. But if the couple hadn't rendezvoused at her apartment, and since his place was obviously out, they'd had to meet somewhere.

She switched on the light and went to jot down a note to herself to follow up on the question, just as she heard something scratch against her window.

Akela froze. Her bedroom was on the second floor with no easy means of access aside from a narrow storm drain. She slowly reached to switch off the light and lay there, watching the window. There was a light breeze tonight and the shadows of the cypress waved on the ceiling. Again, the scratching sounded.

She took off the chain she wore around her neck

at home that held the key to the heavy nightstand and unlocked the drawer, reaching for her service gun. With slow movements, she crept toward the window, flicking off the safety on the gun and staying well to the side, out of the sightline of anyone outside. Her heart thudding thickly in her chest, she held the pistol out in front of her, using the end of the barrel to nudge the curtains out of the way.

A branch swayed, scratching across the glass and nearly causing Akela to jump out of her skin.

She dropped the gun to her side and closed her eyes, damning her overactive imagination. What had she thought? That merely by thinking about the killer he'd appear outside her bedroom window?

She'd never really bought into the hocus-pocus and the voodoo connected to her hometown, but she had to admit that this case was beginning to get to her.

She began to straighten the curtains when a shadow of what looked like a man moved across the back lawn. She caught her breath, straining to see better. But whether it had been a man or another dark shadow caused by the wind and moon would remain forever a mystery, because she didn't see it again.

16

"WE'VE GOT A LINE on Lafitte."

Akela had awakened that morning not having slept well and more agitated than she'd ever been, thereby completely unprepared for Detective Alan Chevalier's pronouncement the following morning.

"What?"

"I said we got a line on Lafitte. He's in the city."

The Eighth District station was abuzz with activity, giving the morning a surreal feeling. Colors seemed somehow more vivid, background noise louder.

Chevalier was shrugging into his ever-present overcoat. "Word came in from one of our snitches this morning. He's at a hotel over on Bourbon Street, close enough to the Hotel Josephine to spit on it."

Akela was familiar with the hotel if only because she was familiar with everything within a quarter mile radius of where Claire Laraway had been murdered.

"How reliable a snitch are we talking about?" she asked, her mood taking a further nosedive.

She'd been ready to confront Chevalier on his policy of ignoring evidence because it didn't support the airtight case he was making against Claude. Now the detective was about to arrest him.

"Reliable enough." He considered her closely. A little too closely. "Why?"

"Seems like a waste of time to dispatch an arrest team if the man is still in the surrounding bayous."

"The information is consistent with some other tips we received yesterday."

Chevalier, along with three other armed detectives, passed her on the way out through the bull pen. She followed them onto the street where two squad cars with uniformed officers were also waiting.

Akela's mind swam with the scene. If she had arrived two minutes later, she would have missed the raid.

"What's the matter, Brooks? I would have thought you'd be happy that we'll finally have the guy who held you hostage."

She climbed into the backseat of his plain sedan, another detective sitting in the front seat next to Chevalier.

"I'm just wondering how reliable this information is. I haven't come across anything that would lead me to indicate that Lafitte was back in the city."

Alan met her gaze in the rearview mirror. "Maybe you've been checking in the wrong places."

Akela focused her attention outside the car, finding it ironic that she could say the same of him but for opposing reasons.

All too soon the sedans sped into place a block up from the hotel in question. Officers, both uniformed and plainclothes, spilled out, the closing of car doors almost rhythmic. In contrast, Akela's heart beat an uneven cadence in her chest as she fingered her cell phone in her pocket.

Three officers rounded to the back of the hotel while Akela followed Chevalier and three others into the lobby, two staying put outside.

Chevalier stayed her with a hand. "Wait here."

Akela stared at him. "I want to be present for the arrest."

"Why? In case I need visual verification? I think I can handle that." He took his firearm out of its holster. "Stay here."

The four men bypassed the elevator and took the stairs up to the left.

Akela paced a short way across the airy lobby, the setup and decor not unlike that of Hotel Josephine in that it was in dire need of renovation. A guy in his early twenties manned the front desk, but as soon as the officers disappeared up the stairs, he quickly stepped into a back room, presumably out of the line of fire.

She paced again, then plopped down on a chair, blowing out a frustrated puff of air. What was the point of bringing her along if he wasn't going to include her in the arrest?

Then again, it probably had never been his intention to bring her along at all. That was why he'd been in a hellfire rush to get out of the station: he'd hoped to be gone by the time she showed up.

Akela crossed her arms and her legs, swinging her foot quickly back and forth as she waited. She checked her watch. If Claude was, indeed, in one of the rooms, then there was very little she could do to help protect him now. She only hoped he didn't put up a fight. Chevalier and his men looked as though they'd be only too happy to shoot him.

CLAUDE PICKED UP the room phone on the first ring.

"They're coming up," said the front desk guy he'd slipped a fifty the night he'd checked in.

He didn't need to ask who was on their way up. He quickly hung up the phone, grabbed his things then climbed from the window of the third-story room. The balcony connected to the other rooms, so it didn't take a great deal of effort to navigate his way three rooms over. He looked down to find three uniformed officers spilling out into the back alley, their guns drawn. He quickly opened the window and let himself inside the empty room, hoping not to be spotted. Once inside, he crossed to the door, pressing his ear to the wood.

"Open up! Police!" someone shouted, then he heard the sound of wood cracking.

A moment later, Claude opened the door a hair, watching as the officers burst into the room where he'd stayed the past couple of nights. That was his cue to come out of the room he stood in and rush the elevator directly across the way.

Unlike many of the hotels in the area, this one had basement access, one of the many reasons he'd chosen it. He stepped in the elevator and pressed the button for that level then stood back out of sight. The elevator ground to a stop at the second floor. Claude closed his eyes and muttered a curse under his breath as a pair of tourists in polyester got in.

"I didn't know it would be so infernally hot here," the woman was saying, looking through her large straw bag for something, then slipping on a pair of sunglasses.

Claude said a quiet prayer as the man pushed the lobby button.

Damn.

He tried to make himself one with the side of the elevator as it drew to a stop and the doors slid open on the lobby level.

The couple stepped out. Just as the doors were sliding shut, he looked out—and met Akela's gaze where she sat in the lobby looking none too happy.

The doors closed.

AKELA SAT FROZEN to the spot, questioning what she'd just seen.

Had Claude really just been on that elevator?

She looked around for any nearby officers, began to get up, nearly ran into the couple that had gotten out of the elevator, then sat back down again.

"Did you see him?"

She blinked up at where Chevalier had just burst back into the lobby from the stairs, noticeably out of breath as he looked wildly around, gun drawn.

Akela debated telling him she'd just seen Claude on the elevator, obviously heading down, but then decided not to if only because she'd then have to explain what she was still doing sitting there.

"No."

"Damn it all to hell."

The rumpled detective strode toward the doors, talking madly into his radio.

"Team two, do you have anything?"

A blip of static then, "No, sir. Nothing out back."

Akela fought the urge to smile as she got up and followed Chevalier back outside, discreetly searching for signs of Claude.

Then she remembered the front deskman and the fact that the detective hadn't approached him. Could he have been the snitch? If so, she had the feeling that the guy had been working both sides of the equation and had given Claude the warning he'd needed to make his escape.

Of course, all she had to do was say the word and the officers now gathering in front of the hotel would refocus their efforts on the lower level of the hotel.

But she remained staunchly silent, figuring it was what Chevalier deserved for trying to cut her out of the arrest.

"MIMI CULPEPPER?"

Akela had been putting off this meeting for as long as she could, not looking forward to talking to a woman both Josie and the strip club owner suspected might have negative things to say about Claude. But as her list of options for proving his innocence shortened, she was forced to look into this lead, hoping against hope that everyone was wrong and that Mimi would give her something she could use.

"What the hell do you want?"

"My name's Akela Brooks. I'm with the FBI."

There was a long silence from the speaker situated outside the front doors to the three-story apartment building near Jackson Square. For a moment, she thought the woman might ignore her. Then she heard the buzz indicating she was being let in. She pushed open the front door and stepped inside the stuffy hall. She took the steps to the third-floor landing and found herself face-to-face with a woman younger than she was.

"Mimi Culpepper?"

"You were expecting somebody else?" she asked, her arms crossed over her chest, an impressive chest in a tight white T-shirt with something written in red glitter that Akela couldn't make out. The shirt combined with snug jeans revealed a body that had been built for stripping. The blonde was stunningly pretty, even if her sneering expression was not.

"I was wondering when they were going to send somebody over here," she said hotly.

Akela frowned as she fished her notepad from her jacket pocket. "They?"

"The police, of course. I called them the day that poor girl was killed."

Akela supposed she should be glad she hadn't

said "the poor girl Claude killed," but she got the distinct impression that that's what Mimi was going to say anyway.

"And no one's been over to take your statement?"

"Nope."

Probably Chevalier would have been there with bells on had he known he was dealing with a prime witness for the prosecution.

"So what is it you have to say that will help in the investigation, Miss Culpepper?"

She blinked at her. "That he did it, of course. Claude Lafitte killed that girl as surely as I'm standing here."

Akela stared at her, a shiver running over her skin despite her suspicion that the woman was lying. "And your reason for thinking that is…"

"I don't just think it, lady, I know it." She pointed to her own neck. "He tried to strangle me."

Akela looked at the neck in question. "And when might this have occurred?"

"Right after sex."

The woman looked a little too smug.

Akela said, "That's not what I meant." She slapped her notebook closed. "At any rate, the victim wasn't strangled."

She debated the wisdom of sharing that tidbit. For all she knew, Mimi Culpepper would put another call into Chevalier and change her story, claim that Claude had tried to slit her throat.

She shivered again, remembering the image of Claire Laraway lying on that hotel bed naked and unmoving.

"Is that it?" the woman asked.

Akela stared at her. "For now."

She turned and walked down the stairs, wondering how Claude had ever thought to get involved with such a scornful woman.

"How can I contact you?"

"You can't," Akela called back up the stairs. "We'll call you."

A COUPLE OF HOURS LATER Akela found herself back at Hotel Josephine. There was something hovering just outside her train of thought that kept drawing her back to the hotel, something she hoped the return visit would help bring out.

Josie didn't appear surprised to see her. Then again, she suspected that Josie was surprised by very little. It was more than just the fact that she owned and ran the hotel; there was an air about her that spoke of a difficult life, a struggle that left her dark eyes wary and her demeanor standoffish.

"Agent Brooks," she said when Akela entered. "What can I do for you today?"

Akela looked around the large lobby. While there wasn't much activity, things appeared to be going slightly better than they had been two days ago. "Just stopping in for a minute to see if you've remembered anything else."

Josie shook her head as she swiped at something on the counter. "Nothing."

Akela watched a couple come down the stairs. "Looks like business has picked back up."

"Tourists who don't know about what went down."

Akela nodded, figuring as much.

"That and one of the ghost tours has started coming by here."

"Oh?" Akela was aware of the nightly walking tours popular with the tourists. New Orleans was known as the ghost capital of the U.S. and some of the local folk took great advantage of the title.

"Yeah. At about nine every night a group stands outside the doors and the guide tells them all about the murder in gruesome detail." Was it her, or had Josie just shuddered? "The Quarter Killer. A story designed to strike the fear of God in young women, you know, seeing as he's still running around loose."

"Don't tell me you've changed your mind about being scared."

Josie stared at her. "I just don't like me or my place being connected to the story."

Akela had the feeling that the murder wasn't the first time the hotel's name had made it into the news, but pretty much every place in New Orleans had a history, so she wasn't about to push the issue.

"I was wondering if anyone thought to ask you about the victim."

Josie waited as Akela took her notepad out of her pocket.

"Do you remember seeing her around before that night?"

Josie looked evasive.

Interesting…

"So you did, then."

Josie shrugged. "Part of what makes me successful is that I don't go around wagging my tongue."

"Even if it means catching the Quarter Killer?"

Josie narrowed her eyes. "Judging by the news, the police are convinced that Claude Lafitte is your man."

"Let's just say some additional evidence has come to light. Now about Claire Laraway…"

Josie sighed as if she would really prefer not to be having this conversation. Akela was struck by how close they'd come to not having it. "She was in here once or twice before that night."

"Which one was it? Once or twice?"

"Four times. She always came alone and rented a room."

"But she didn't stay alone."

She shrugged. "I wouldn't know. I never saw her with anyone."

"But you strike me as the type that knows what's going on at all times in her place of business."

"So I am."

"The man she met…"

Josie held up her hands. "Look, I never really got a close look, you know? He always came in when I was busy with other customers and snuck up the stairs." She was absently rubbing her arm. "The same when he left."

Akela tried to decipher whether or not she was telling the truth. "You sure?"

"Positive."

She sighed. If the guy Claire had met here was the same 'C' from her diary—and Akela was sure he was—she wasn't surprised that he would go to extra lengths not to be noticed.

"You know, you really should consider getting some security cameras put up in here," Akela said. "A city like this isn't safe for a girl, even a capable one like you."

"Tell me about it. But right now I'm trying to

figure out how I'm going to cover my tax bill, much less afford security cameras."

Point taken.

Akela pocketed her notepad, absently wondering what she was going to do with the information she had compiled, information that could easily be used to deflect suspicion from Claude, bitter Mimi Culpepper aside. But was it enough? Could Claude be cleared without the real killer being caught?

"Agent?"

"Please, call me Akela."

"Was there anything else?"

"Hmm? Oh, no. I guess not." She slid another of her business cards across the counter. "Should you remember anything about the man, or Miss Laraway, or anything at all…please call me. I'll make sure the info can't be traced back to you."

Josie picked up the card and tucked it in her pocket as if merely having it out on the counter was proof of some sort of guilt. "I will."

Akela knew she wouldn't, but there was little she could do about that. Until, when and if she had any additional questions, their conversation would end there.

17

LATELY, NIGHTS WERE Akela's least favorite time. Everyone but her was asleep. She couldn't follow up on clues. Essentially she felt like a prisoner of the darkness, her movements restricted, her options limited. And, of course, it didn't help that even though Claude had physically released her days ago, emotionally she was still very much his hostage.

She lay across her big, empty bed, the light from the moon cutting a swatch of dim, blue light across her midsection. She really could use some sleep, but the peaceful escape eluded her like a thief in the night. Her mind clicked with everything that had happened that day—from Mimi Culpepper's acidic bitterness, to Claude's softly spoken erotic commands over the phone in the wee hours. Her brain refused to shut down.

She absently fingered the corner of the pillow next to her, feeling out of sorts. That restlessness might have scared her had she not been in the middle of an investigation, even though she suspected that same agitation had very little to do with Claire Laraway's murder, and everything to do with the man accused of murdering her.

Against her better judgment, she'd given herself over to the need to call him earlier, to make sure he was all right. He hadn't picked up. The experience had left her even more worried. She wouldn't put it past Chevalier to keep another arrest attempt from her. And although she was pretty sure Claude wasn't in the county lockup, there was more she was concerned about than the risk of his arrest.

She wasn't sure when exactly her desire for brief, no-strings-attached sex with the hot Cajun had morphed into something more, but she was positive that was what lay at the core of her restlessness. She knew a hunger for him that went beyond sex and beyond what he could do to her with a few whispered suggestive words. When she wasn't with him, she yearned to be with him. There didn't seem to be a single moment that went by that she wasn't thinking about him and, oddly enough, most of the thoughts had absolutely no connection to the case. She wanted to know what the first sentence he'd ever written was. What his first pair of shoes were. Whether or not he'd gone to his senior prom and whom he'd gone with. She wanted to see pictures of him missing his front teeth, and share memories of his upbringing. She knew his mother had died some years back and that the space on his birth certificate had read John Doe, but did he share an emotional closeness with the woman who had raised him or had they always been at loggerheads like her and her mother?

And, mostly, she was afraid that she'd never get the chance to have any of her questions answered, not only because he was facing murder charges, but because Jean-Claude Lafitte wasn't a man made for marriage or long-term relationships. He was someone who lived fully in the here and now, who followed his urges and didn't know the meaning of the word restraint.

Meanwhile she had spent almost the whole of her twenty-eight years reacting to events rather than making them happen.

Akela closed her eyes and swallowed hard. As difficult as it was to face, that's who she was. Her cautiousness and natural care made her a damn good FBI agent.

It also made her a scared and lonely woman.

She felt a light touch on her arm. Goose bumps swept along her skin and she went still, fear coalescing in her stomach.

"Shh, *chere,* no reason to be afraid."

Claude.

She lay quietly, wondering if the touch and his words were a figment of her imagination or if, indeed, he had somehow managed to gain access to the well-protected house and approach her bed without her hearing him.

The top sheet lifted from her body and a moment later she felt weight on the mattress next to her, then Claude's warm, naked body curved against hers.

Akela stifled a moan, the combination of her chaotic thoughts and yearnings coming together to make her acutely aware of the man who had snuck into her bed and her heart when she wasn't looking.

"I was hoping to catch you before you came home, but I didn't. So when I saw through the window that you'd come into your room…I hope you don't mind my gaining entrance from the back and coming up here. I couldn't help myself."

She reached behind her back, finding his hand on her hip and giving it a squeeze by way of an answer.

"A man couldn't hope for a warmer welcome," he murmured against her ear.

She arched her back, putting her gown-covered bottom in direct contact with his obvious arousal. All her worries evaporated, leaving nothing but sheer want in their wake.

"I'm glad you came," she whispered.

He snaked his hand up to her chin and turned her face toward him. "I'm glad you're glad."

He kissed her lingeringly, his mouth warm, his lips insistent.

Akela shifted to roll over and he held her still.

"Non, *ma catin*. I want you to stay like this."

She thought she might cry out with the need to hold him, to feel him in her arms—until his hand ran over her alert breasts, down her midsection, then straight to the crux of her desire for him. She lifted her leg so that it curved over his, giving him better access. Slowly he raised the hem of her nightgown, until it brushed the top of her thighs, revealing her to him. He grabbed her swollen flesh almost roughly, as if he'd been longing to touch her as much as she'd been longing to be touched. Then his finger was inside the leg of her panties and he was stroking her hot slickness.

Akela threw her head back and moaned, shooting sensations traveling across her skin, making her shiver all over.

"I want you so badly I don't think I can wait," he whispered, kissing the side of her throat.

"Who's asking you to wait?"

Then just like that he was stripping her panties

from her, sheathing himself in a condom, then lifting her leg to gain access to her from behind.

Akela nearly climaxed at the first stroke of his hardness against her exposed flesh. But rather than immediately entering her, as she so wanted him to, he slid his erection back and forth, over her clit then down again, creating a hot, wet friction that left her panting.

"Please," she whispered.

He snaked his other hand under her and held her still when she might have bore back on him. Pulling her nightgown up farther, he found her breast and gave an almost painful squeeze, forcing the air from her lungs in a surprised whoosh.

Then he entered her in one long, hard stroke that left her little more than a puddle of quivering, convulsing flesh.

Akela had never come so quickly and the reality left her feeling exquisitely, blessedly alive. At the same time as she pressed against him, she realized he'd gone very, very still, as if fending off his own climax. She shuddered against him, reveling in the feel of his fingers against her breast, his arousal between her legs. Every part of her seemed to pulse and vibrate as she drew herself down his length slowly, then slid back again, starting a rhythm he had yet to follow as he clutched her hip in his other hand.

"You're going to be the death of me," he groaned in her ear.

He rolled her so she was on her stomach, then pulled her hips so that she was up on her knees. Akela scrambled to keep her balance with her hands, bracing herself for him when he thrust into her long and hard from behind.

She dropped her chin to her chest and moaned, incredible, molten pleasure lapping like waves over her body. His fingers clutched her hips almost harshly, holding her still, holding her fast as he withdrew from her, stroking her swollen flesh with his thick length. Just when she might cry out for a deeper meeting, he surged into her again, his skin slapping against hers as he thrust again, and again.

Akela was half-afraid she might spontaneously combust. She bore backward and worked her hips forward, stroking him as he stroked her. They found an even rhythm that made her soar higher with each meeting, back and forth, in and out....

Then he slid his hand down over her hip and between her legs, catching her clit between his finger and thumb and squeezing, shattering her into a thousand tiny sparkling pieces, his deep, low groan indicating he'd followed right after her.

She collapsed to the mattress with him still inside her and he lay against her, his breathing heavy in her ear, his fingers still idly caressing her so she felt as if she had no power over her shuddering body.

"I keep waiting for my interest in you to wane," he said quietly, moving her hair from the back of her neck with his nose, then nipping the sensitive skin. "Instead my want for you only grows."

Akela understood all too well what he was saying. Casual sex was supposed to be, by its very nature, meaningless. But she found nothing superficial about how she felt when she made love to him. When he touched her. When he stroked her inside and out, setting her soul on fire.

He gently rolled off of her, drawing her against the length of his body and smoothing her hair.

And it was there, in the strength and warmth of his arms, that Akela finally found the peace she'd been seeking for what seemed like her entire life.

AKELA WAS AWARE of warmth spreading along her skin. In the cotton web of her dream, she surged toward it, opening herself to the addictive heat. Her eyelids fluttered open only to discover that it wasn't a dream at all, but delicious reality. The early-morning sun shone through her bedroom window, bathing her in light, while Claude was running his tongue along the tight bud of her breast, as if seeking sustenance only she could provide.

"Good morning," he said.

And a very good morning it was, too. Akela felt as if she'd been reborn somehow, her body both drained and sated, although Claude's skillful attentions were igniting desire in her all over again.

"Hello yourself," she murmured, entwining her fingers in his thick, tousled hair, the strands coarse against her skin.

He dipped his head lower, lapping the skin of her stomach, making her draw in a quick breath.

"Has anyone ever told you you're insatiable?" She pressed her head back into the pillows and closed her eyes, overly aware of the smile on her face. She blindly reached to cover his mouth. "No, don't answer that."

He chuckled quietly and she removed her hand. He took advantage of his new freedom by burying his nose in the wedge of curls between her legs, burrowing until he nipped at her core with his lips.

Akela gasped, her back coming up off the bed at the shock of sensation.

Long, shuddering moments later, she stared at Claude through the fringe of her lashes, wondering how many times he'd brought her to climax throughout the night. She'd lost count at somewhere around the fifth time, merely going with the flow.

She scooted down on the linens, reaching for the proof of his arousal. He caught her hand.

"It's getting late."

She turned her head to look at the clock. It was after seven.

She nearly jackknifed up off the bed. Her glorious awakening had made her oblivious to where she was and what time it was.

Claude held her still. "It's not that late."

He got up from the bed in all his nude glory, stepping to the connecting bathroom.

Akela smiled and stretched out, identifying muscles she hadn't been aware she had. She heard the sound of the shower, knowing she should be getting up herself, should be picking up the pillows and covers that had fallen from the bed during the night, but she couldn't do anything more than lie there, basking in the aftermath of their lovemaking session.

She heard a door click open and she propped herself up on her elbows. Only it wasn't the bathroom door that had opened, but rather the door to the hall. And it wasn't Claude she was looking at, but her four-year-old daughter, Daisy.

Akela immediately covered herself with the top sheet.

"Mommy, Mommy!"

"Daisy, honey! What are you doing up so early?"

She couldn't remember the last time her daughter had burst into her room like that. Surely it had been well before they'd moved back to New Orleans.

The four-year-old was all smiles and tangled blond hair in her pink nightgown and slippers. "Grandma, I mean Grandmother said that you might like to have breakfast with us."

Then the bathroom door did open and Claude stepped out, only a towel wrapped around his hips, rubbing another towel against his damp hair, both mother and daughter gaping at him.

"Did somebody say breakfast?" he asked.

18

AKELA SLIPPED INTO her robe and knelt in front of her daughter, taking her hands. "Daisy, honey, why don't you go downstairs and help set the table for breakfast?"

Claude watched the exchange, noticing the complete one-eighty Akela had made since he'd left her to take a shower. She seemed tense and worried. And she'd positioned herself so that her daughter couldn't see him, although the little cherub kept peering over her shoulder at him curiously.

"Do you like eggs?" the girl asked him.

Akela appeared at a loss for words, her gaze going from him to her daughter.

Whatever joy Claude had felt at seeing Akela's daughter for the first time ebbed at the look of almost panic on her beautiful face.

Akela said finally, "Mr. Lafitte won't be staying for breakfast, honey."

Daisy looked disappointed. But she couldn't have

been any more disappointed than Claude was as he watched Akela steer her daughter from the room.

He rubbed the towel he held against his hair with more pressure than was needed. What had he expected? Last night hadn't been some pajama party with pancakes waiting on the table for them in the morning. He was still wanted for murder. And Akela was still a law-enforcement agent whose job it was to arrest him.

She came back into the room, her cheeks flushed, her eyes overly bright. And Claude understood in that one moment that everything they'd been trying to avoid, all that they'd ignored, had just hit them both full in the face, causing the crack that had always been between them to gape wide-open.

"I…I need to get dressed," she said quietly, then passed him to close herself in the bathroom.

AKELA FINISHED applying her makeup, checked her hair one last time, then collapsed onto the closed commode.

She was surprised to find herself out of breath. Ever since Claude had come out of the bathroom and Daisy had seen him, she'd been on overdrive, desperately searching for a way to turn back the hands of time so that reality wasn't staring at her with bleak intensity.

Her time with Claude on the bayou had been like a dream, something separate from her day-to-day life. And when they'd come in contact again in the city, she'd allowed that same sense of the unreal to blur the here and now.

Only it wasn't a dream, was it? What had developed between her and Claude was much more than that. Deeper. More complicated.

She rested her head in her hands and tightly closed her eyes.

She'd been through this before, having engaged in a secret affair with her ex-partner. Although the reasons for hiding her relationship with Dan had been completely different than those in operation now—namely the strict FBI policy of no personal relations between agents—she couldn't help drawing a parallel between the two liaisons. Her feelings for both men had developed in a vacuum, outside her normal life, outside public opinion and rational thought and practical applications.

And in Dan's case she'd figured out fairly quickly that what they'd shared in the dark hadn't had what it took to make it in the light of day, despite the birth of their daughter.

Only Claude wasn't Dan, was he? He wasn't her professional partner. Worse, he was a fugitive on the run from the law. And she was the law.

And Daisy's walking into her bedroom had brought that all home like a fist to the chest.

She pushed from the toilet, straightening the waist of her navy-blue slacks then smoothing the lapels of the matching jacket. She stared at the woman in the mirror, unfamiliar to her now in a way that almost frightened her. This no-nonsense, official-looking person was miles away from the woman she'd been the night before. The woman who had willingly engaged in an affair with a fugitive.

A fugitive who she was in love with.

She opened the bathroom door to find Claude sitting on the side of her bed, fully dressed. His gaze was trained on her carpet, his hands clasped between his knees.

Akela's heart did a painful flip in her chest.

"So," he said quietly. "I guess that's it, then."

She was bowled over that he seemed to be having the same thoughts as she was.

She didn't know what to say, so she said nothing. In fact, she wondered if she was capable of saying anything at all given the tightness of her throat and the burning sensation behind her eyes.

He rose from the bed and collected his cell phone from the nightstand. "Just so you know, I plan on surrendering to the authorities this morning."

She opened her mouth to object, recognizing

that the knee-jerk reaction was in direct contrast to what she'd been recommending to him all along.

"Why now?" she whispered.

"Come on, Akela, we both know it's only a matter of time. How many front deskmen can I pay to tip me off about a raid? I've hit a roadblock."

But you're innocent, she wanted to say.

She felt his gaze on her and blinked up to find him staring at her with his heart in his eyes. And she felt her own heart break.

"I," he said, then cleared his throat, "I don't think it would be a good idea if I ran into anyone else. Is there a back way out of here?"

Akela felt a lone tear slash a path down her cheek. She quickly wiped it away with the back of her hand and nodded. "Yes. But it's through the kitchen. And my family…"

He looked away. "Maybe it would be better for me to go out the front then."

He walked toward the door.

Akela automatically moved behind him, silently following him down the stairs, uncaring of who saw her and what they might think. Not seeing anything but the man who was walking not only out of her house, but her life.

All too soon they came to the front door. She reached out and touched his shoulder.

"Let me come with you to the station."

He shook his head. "No. I've already caused enough trouble for you. I won't be the cause of any more."

"Please," she said, putting her arms around him and holding him tight.

He smelled of her bath soap, of laundry detergent and somehow of the bayou, although the last was probably her imagination since she'd always associate him with that magical locale.

His arms slowly went around her, his hands resting on the small of her back as he pressed her even closer. He buried his face in the side of her neck, seeming to breathe her in much as she was him.

"Ah, *chere*. It seems love is not without a sense of humor."

Love?

She shifted to look into his eyes, only the instant she moved, he took advantage of her letting go of him to turn and go.

He opened the door and an ominous series of metallic clicks sounded. Akela froze when she saw three uniformed officers, headed up by Detective Chevalier, their guns trained on Claude.

"Jean-Claude Lafitte, you are under arrest."

19

No GOOD DEED goes unpunished.

Claude thought of the saying as he sat in the holding cell with some fifteen other men, each waiting for his bail hearing to be called.

Of course, he had never had the chance to do a good deed. He hadn't surrendered to authorities. Instead, the authorities had found him first—and at Akela's of all places.

He rubbed his hands roughly against his face.

He wasn't sure what bothered him more: being arrested for a crime he didn't commit, or the memory of Akela's expression that morning when they'd both realized that they'd reached the end of the road.

Only that road had ended even more abruptly when he'd opened the door to leave her.

He jerked upright, leaning his back against the wall and staring blindly forward, ignoring the guy next to him who was trying to hit him up for a cigarette. He'd known the instant he'd kissed her out at the bayou that he should never have started something with her while he was still a wanted man. It had been that knowledge that had provided him with the strength he'd needed to drive her back to the city, no matter the risk to himself.

But it had been that same kiss that had ignited in him a want of her that went beyond physical need.

Four days ago he would never have considered turning himself over to authorities. And he would never have risked what he had last night by going to her place, the desire to see her so strong that he'd put both of their lives on the line. He'd been blinded by something that had made him push that danger aside if only to kiss her again. And it was that something that made him feel uncomfortable in his own skin now.

He loved her.

The realization didn't come as a shock to him. While he hadn't outwardly acknowledged it before, he supposed he'd been aware enough while it was happening. He'd probably fallen for her that first day at the cabin as she'd lain handcuffed to the bed in nothing but her slip looking like temptation incarnate. If not then, he'd certainly been far gone when he'd made love to her the first time. There had been something different about their coming together. Something more powerful than he'd experienced before. Something that soured him against any other woman because that which he sought lay solely with Akela.

Of course, recognizing his feelings for her now did him no good at all. He faced what could be a lifetime in prison, if not death by lethal injection.

But above and beyond that, he hated that he'd brought trouble to Akela's life.

He looked around his depressing surroundings. Thierry had warned him that he was heading for a fall. Little did his brother know that the fall that hurt the most was one that had nothing to do with his being in jail.

THE NOPD HAD BEEN watching her house.

Akela paced down the length of the Eighth District station hall and back again, recalling the times she'd felt as if she was being watched, the times she'd written the sensation off as something coming from within rather than without, the times she'd thought Claude, himself, might have been watching her. Instead it had been an undercover officer with the NOPD.

And now Claude was in jail.

She finally spotted Alan Chevalier walking to his office and headed in the lead detective's direction, battling back both guilt and indignation.

"What's the deal with having me watched?" she demanded, entering his office behind him then slamming the door.

The rumpled homicide detective shrugged out of his overcoat and hung it on the back of his door.

"Interestingly enough, I was doing it for your safety."

Akela crossed her arms.

"After you were taken hostage, I figured it would be a good idea to keep an eye on you, make sure you were safe."

"No, you used me as bait."

His barely concealed smile told her she was right. "And I caught a big one, didn't I?"

"And you've made a big mistake."

He checked some papers on his desk, then looked at her. "No, Agent Brooks, I'd say you're the one who's made the mistake."

"Tell me this, Alan. What will the court of public opinion make of the evidence you chose to ignore in your one-track mission to pin this murder on Lafitte?"

"I didn't have to pin anything on him. He did it."

"Then you won't have a problem with my going to the prosecutor with the information that Claire Laraway was having an affair with a married lover who obviously wasn't happy with some things she'd been doing—like talking to his wife, and sleeping with another man."

Alan's hands tightened on the back of his chair.

"Or how about the fact that there's a key piece of evidence that doesn't belong to either the victim or Lafitte that was found in the victim's wound, possibly placed there on purpose?"

She didn't miss his smirk. "Sex has made you go soft in the head, Brooks. What's to say Lafitte didn't plant that evidence himself?"

"Awfully premeditated for a crime of passion, isn't it?"

Akela's throat tightened as everything she'd been afraid would happen was unfolding right in front of her eyes. And there was nothing she could do to stop it.

"How long have you been meeting the suspect in private?"

"How long have you been watching me?"

He waved a hand. "Since you were set free."

Oh, God…

"But only at night. We figured that was probably when Lafitte might make contact." He opened then closed a drawer. "Besides, the department couldn't afford more than that."

Relief flooded Akela's tense muscles.

He grinned at her. "From what I understand,

we got some interesting videotape last night,
though."

The relief vanished…and in its place came a
thought.

"Where are you going?" Chevalier demanded.

She spared him a look. "You wouldn't be interested because it has nothing to do with building a
case against Lafitte."

AKELA STOOD in the middle of the street where everything had begun six short days earlier: Bourbon
Street in the French Quarter. In the exact spot where
she'd literally bumped into Claude Lafitte. Before
she'd known who he was. Before he'd become a
suspect in Claire Laraway's murder. Before he'd
opened up a world to her she'd never known existed.

Her cell phone vibrated. She checked it to find
Chevalier trying to reach her. She ignored him.

It was hard to remember they were working for
the same team. Of course, Chevalier didn't have
the personal interest in the case that she did. And
she understood that he believed Claude had seduced her toward the end of gaining her trust and
faith. And, truth be told, a part of her wondered if
that was, in fact, the case.

But as a trained federal agent, she'd learned to
trust her gut instincts. And her instincts in this case

told her that Claude Lafitte was one hundred percent innocent of the crime of which he was accused.

A case of her heart ruling her head?

Perhaps.

But she'd operated so hard, for so long, with
only her head that she had to give her heart—and
Claude—a chance, no matter the consequences.

She walked a few steps, visually scanning the
businesses around Hotel Josephine. She noticed
the young owner was standing just outside the
front door to her establishment, wearing a white
linen dress that should have made her look plain,
instead clinging to her curvy body in all the right
places. She crossed her arms over her chest, watching Akela with hooded interest.

Her cell phone vibrated again. Out of habit, she
checked it, expecting to see the detective trying to
contact her again. Instead it was her mother.

She answered on the third ring.

"I cannot believe you brought a known fugitive—a murderer—into our house," Patsy Brooks
said in an even tone.

"Mother, I can't talk to you now."

"What do you want me to do, Akela Lynn?
Schedule an appointment to speak with my own
daughter?"

A car honked its horn. Akela stepped out of the

way to let it pass, her gaze continuing to take in her surroundings. "No, Mother, that's not necessary."

"Then do you mind explaining to me what happened here this morning?"

"What happened is that I'm a grown woman and I had a guest over."

"A guest? Is that what they're calling killers now?"

"Claude isn't a killer."

"According to whom? I knew the instant I saw him coming down the stairs who he was, Akela. He kidnapped you, for God's sake! And you let him into our house. Allowed him contact with my granddaughter."

Akela's gaze settled on what she was looking for. Bingo.

"Don't worry, Mother. Daisy and I will be moving out by month's end."

Silence. Then, "You can't."

"Why can't I?" Akela asked as she stepped across the street from the Hotel Josephine, her gaze on something attached to the roof of a popular bar. "Look, Mother, you understood that I moved back not because of financial concerns—my job pays me well—but for issues having to do with family. And you said you didn't have a problem with treating me like an adult."

"I don't."

"Yes, you do. The first time I do something as an adult and you're taking me to task for it." She heaved a sigh. "Look, I really can't have this conversation right now. I'll talk to you when I get home."

She disconnected the call just as a young man in a waiter's uniform came out of the business she stood in front of.

"This camera," she said, pointing to the object in question. "Is it running all the time?"

He nodded.

She flashed her ID. "Can you go get your boss for me, please?"

ALAN CHEVALIER sat back in his office chair, feet up on his desk, lighting a cigar from a box he kept reserved for special occasions. His co-workers were crowded into the small space and spilled out through the open door, talking about Lafitte's arrest and the end to a case that had garnered the station more than a little unwanted attention.

Not to mention the attention Alan, himself, had gotten from his immediate superior, Captain Seymour Hodge, who had made it clear that if Alan didn't catch the Quarter Killer, his fifteen-year career was dead.

He stared at the glowing end of his cigar, trying to recapture the triumph he'd felt when he'd slapped the handcuffs on Jean-Claude Lafitte's wrists, but it eluded him; instead Akela Brooks's accusations trailed through his mind.

He was aware of the trace evidence found on the victim pointing to a third person being in that hotel room. Was aware and had purposely ignored it in light of no other evidence pointing to another suspect. Was what she'd said true? Could Claire Laraway have been dating a married man and begun making life miserable for her lover?

He thought of the reason his job had been ceaselessly on the line for the past ten months, more specifically, the instant his superior's estranged wife had let her husband know in a very public display of anger that she and Alan had had sex.

He better than anyone knew the ends a spurned or vengeful lover could go to in order to reap her revenge. Or, if Akela was right and the married man might have committed the crime, *his* revenge.

"Hey, Lieutenant, does this mean you're going to have time to get your clothes pressed at the cleaners and buy a razor?" one of the junior detectives called out.

The room filled with laughter.

"Better yet, I think we should all chip in and buy him an iron."

The men began taking dollar bills out of their pockets and flinging them at his desk.

Alan grinned and rocked back slightly in his chair.

The room suddenly fell silent. He saw why when Captain Seymour Hodge, District Commander, appeared in the middle of the sea of people that had parted.

"Chevalier. In my office. Now."

Hodge left and Alan sat for a long moment, his co-workers' uneasy attention on him. He puffed absently on his cigar, then let his feet drop to the floor.

"Uh-oh. Looks like more trouble in paradise," one of the detectives said.

Nobody laughed at that crack as Alan snuffed out his cigar in an ashtray, then got to his feet. He had the feeling this wasn't going to be pretty.

He got a flash of just how ugly things were going to get when he rapped on Hodge's door then stepped inside the office to find Akela Brooks and the city prosecutor, Bill Grissom, standing alongside the stone-faced captain.

20

AKELA FELT as if she was back in law school re-playing that mock trial she had lost all those years ago when she'd tried to prove the innocence of an accused man.

Only now there was nothing mock about what was happening. And the defendant wasn't some fictional character, but Claude, who was even now sitting behind bars with her as his only hope of ever being on the other side of them.

"Come in, Detective," Captain Hodge said.

The captain was maybe two, three years older than Chevalier. And as a result of some of the in-station investigating she'd done, she understood that the two men had been friends. Once. A place they would never get back to again, if past events were an accurate indicator. That's what happened when you made the mistake of getting friendly with a man's estranged wife.

Akela had relied on the bad blood to set the

stage for what she'd already shown to the prosecutor, Bill Grissom, and Captain Seymour Hodge.

Alan closed the door after himself. "What's going on?"

"Agent Brooks has just been sharing some interesting information with us."

Akela stood with her hands clasped behind her back as the detective stared at her.

"Yes, well, has Agent Brooks also filled you in on the fact that she and Lafitte have had personal relations?"

Grissom cleared his throat. "Yes, she has."

"But that's not why we're here," Akela said quickly, not wanting to relive one of the most difficult hours of her life.

She'd known she would be facing an uphill battle when she'd called the prosecutor and the captain and asked to meet with them jointly, mainly because her first item of business would be to address the rumors of her and Claude's personal association. Only they weren't just rumors. They were the truth.

As was Claude's innocence.

She released her hands from behind her back. "What is at issue is the way this investigation was run from the moment the suspect now in custody was found outside the victim's hotel room."

Alan cracked a smile. "You mean the moment you tried to apprehend the suspect and he took you hostage?"

"Keep quiet, Chevalier," the captain said.

Akela took that as her cue. "First, there was the blind eye turned to crime scene evidence—namely, the presence of trace evidence linking a third person to the scene."

"The hair sample," the prosecutor said, nodding.

"Yes," Akela said, warming to her subject. "Next, there was the fact that the victim was involved with someone who had motive for wanting her dead."

Alan rolled his eyes. "This is all circumstantial."

The captain stared at him. "Let the woman speak."

"Why? So she can make a case for her lover?"

Grissom said, "No, so she can free an innocent man from jail."

Akela felt a spark of hope and quickly continued. "And last, but certainly not least, there's the videotape I've secured of the hotel from that morning."

Alan looked at her. "What videotape?"

She stepped to the side to reveal a media unit set up in the corner. "Something the detective said this morning made me consider an angle I hadn't before. Namely that while the Hotel Josephine didn't have a security camera running the morning of the murder, that neighboring businesses might have." She picked up a remote, pushed the button to switch on the television, then started a video playback. "This is footage I obtained from a bar across the street from the hotel."

The image was grainy at best, but it was clear enough to show that the wide-angle camera lens had a clean shot of Bourbon Street and of the hotel, a timeline clock running in the bottom right-hand corner of the screen. They watched as Claude came out of the hotel, walking in the direction he'd been going when Akela had run into him.

Alan snorted. "That only places the suspect at the scene."

Akela held up a hand, then pushed the pause button. "What else does it show, Detective?"

Alan stepped closer to the television set. "Nothing."

"Look a little closer."

There, in a second-floor window was the victim herself, very much alive, opening the window and leaning out, apparently smiling, using a sheet to cover herself.

"Jesus H. Christ," Alan muttered under his breath.

Grissom said, "So that leaves the victim alive

when Lafitte left the hotel that morning, supporting his claim."

Alan swiveled around. "He must have forgotten something and gone back."

"What?" Captain Hodge asked. "Did he forget to kill her?"

Akela pushed the button for the video to continue. A figure in a black raincoat, hat and gloves entered the hotel. From that angle, and given the distance of the shot, it was hard to tell if it was a man or a woman. But what was very clear was that the guest was temporary, going into the hotel, then leaving some minutes later, very obviously in a hurry.

Akela pressed Pause again. "That, gentlemen, is our Quarter Killer."

"Oh, come on," Chevalier said. "You can't buy this load of crap. The killer is in jail as we speak."

"No he's not," Captain Hodge said. "I've put an order through to release him."

"What? You can't be serious?"

The prosecutor rubbed his chin. "He's very serious." He shrugged. "In light of the evidence Agent Brooks has produced, in addition to other details she has meticulously charted, there's not enough for me to prosecute Jean-Claude Lafitte for the murder of Claire Laraway."

"LAFITTE!" barked a guard.

Claude glanced toward the iron bars across the room to find the uniformed officer opening the door. He got up, not looking forward to appearing in front of a judge. The proceeding would only make everything that much more real.

"Has my attorney arrived?" he asked the officer as he held out his hands to be cuffed.

The officer ignored him, closed the door, then stepped down the hall toward the booking room.

Claude followed, staring at his uncuffed hands.

The officer stood at a counter, filling in some paperwork he then pushed in Claude's direction. "Sign here."

Claude looked at the documentation. "Is this something my attorney should see first?"

"You're being sprung, Lafitte. If I were you, I wouldn't look a gift horse in the mouth, boy."

Claude quickly read over the document, discovering that it was, indeed, a release form.

He signed it.

"Here." The officer handed him a large Ziploc bag that apparently held his personal articles, then he motioned toward the door. "You're free to go."

Claude emerged from the county lockup, blinking at the bright midday sun where it hung high in the sky. One word, and one word only came to mind—or, more specifically, a name. Akela.

21

CLAUDE FOUND IT hard to believe that nearly two weeks had passed since he'd been released from custody with no formal charges brought against him related to Claire's murder. His own attorney had been surprised by the move and hadn't been able to explain it, but had counseled Claude not to get too comfortable, if only because the actual murderer had yet to be arrested.

What intrigued Claude more was that the past fourteen days had been more difficult than the time he'd spent on the run and in the county lockup, mostly because he'd gone without seeing Akela.

He paddled his well-worn, handmade kayak over the bayou waters, watching as a cottonmouth snake eased along the surface a few feet away and a kingfisher flew overhead. There didn't seem to be a minute that went by that he didn't think about her—remember her quiet moans…the taste of her essence on his tongue…the vision of her lying in bed next to him, her soft skin against his…and wonder if he'd ever have the chance to touch her again.

He'd thought about calling her to at least thank her for doing whatever she had to spring him. Though she hadn't completely cleared his name, she done enough to gain him his freedom so he might further investigate the case himself to ensure he never saw the inside of a lockup again. Now that he once again had access to his financial resources, and his purchase of Lafitte's Louisiana Boats and Tours was complete, he had two private investigators checking into Claire Laraway's past, trying to determine who would want to kill her and leave him to hang for the crime.

So his life was back on track. The problem was, he was no longer sure it was the track he wanted to be on. Oh, he still wanted the business, even had plans to expand it. Then again, it wasn't so much the track, but the person who was missing from it.

Akela…

He headed for the shore near his cabin. He didn't like that things had ended between them the way they had. Then again, he'd suspected all along that they would end badly. How could it be otherwise considering the circumstances? A fugitive on the run, wanted for murder. A sexy FBI agent who had been caught in his seductive web. Nowhere in the scenario was there room for happily-ever-after.

He steadied the kayak and stepped out into the shallow water, hauling the boat up to shore with him after placing the paddle inside. He'd long stopped challenging the voice that asked him if he'd really been interested in a long-term relationship with the conservative federal agent. There were some things, he was coming to understand, that couldn't be questioned. And love was one of them.

Unfortunately, the woman he chose to fall in love with was the one woman he could never have.

He grimaced, taking off his wet boots and walking toward the cabin. The sun was slanting against the porch and for a minute he thought he saw Akela standing there at the top of the stairs. He rubbed his eyes with his free hand, thinking he'd been out on the water too long—or, more precisely, gone without her for much too long.

"Hi."

He hadn't been imagining things. There, wearing a pretty flowered dress and the kind of strappy red sandals that were designed to turn anyone's head, her brown hair curling around her beautiful face, was Akela.

Claude drew to a stop at the bottom of the stairs, remembering every precious moment they'd spent together. He hadn't even dared hope that she might be willing to reenter his life once his innocence was proven. Only his dreams had conjured up the vision he was seeing.

He didn't know what to say. So he said nothing.

Akela looked suddenly uncomfortable. "I, um, went by your place in the city a couple of times," she said, looking everywhere but at him. "I figured you'd probably come out here to get your feet back under you." She gestured toward the kayak. "That's something I've always wanted to try."

Claude still couldn't find words to say to her. He hefted his boots on top of the steps then rolled up his jeans a couple of turns.

"What are you doing here, Akela?"

He was as surprised by his question as she apparently was, and was even more startled by the brusque way it had come out.

"I…" she trailed off.

He climbed the steps and stood directly in front of her, the heels she wore putting her almost nose to nose with him. Looking at her, he wanted her more than he wanted his next breath.

Unable to suppress the urge any longer, he curved his hand around to the back of her neck and hauled her to him for a kiss—one that was harsher than he'd intended and that was filled with all the emotions twisting in his stomach.

She made a strangled sound and he broke off, staring at her eyes wide with shock.

The screen door hinges squeaked behind her. Claude blinked, for a moment shoved back in time when Akela had been there for professional rather than personal reasons. Had new evidence surfaced? Had she come to arrest him again? To finally put him behind bars and throw away the key?

His heart turned over in his chest as he looked down at the four-year-old who stood next to Akela, taking her mother's hand in her smaller one.

Akela cleared her throat. "Claude, I'd like you to meet my daughter, Daisy. Daisy, this is Mr. Claude."

He crouched down so he was at eye level with the girl. "Well, hello, Miss Daisy. What a nice surprise it is to see you here."

The little girl was all blond curls and smiles. "Mommy and I are making you breakfast."

Every brick Claude had used to defend himself against Akela, the wall he'd erected to protect her from him, crumbled away, leaving him strangely exposed and vulnerable to these two women—two amazing ladies who were much more than a man like him would ever deserve.

"Daisy, honey," Akela said, her voice thick, "why don't you go in and arrange the place settings?"

"Okay!"

The four-year-old rushed for the door, which clapped shut after she went inside.

One of the hardest things Claude had ever done in his life was rise to his feet to face Akela.

"I'm…"

He was what? Sorry? An apology seemed to fall way short of the mark when it came to how he'd been handling this.

Then the significance of not only Akela's appearance, but her show of faith by bringing her daughter with her, hit him full force in the solar plexus.

"I know this, our visit, must come as a shock to you, Claude," Akela whispered, her moist silver eyes revealing the demons she, herself, must be battling. "I'd hoped that what we shared was more…well, more than just sex."

Claude suddenly couldn't breathe.

"I…well, the simple truth of it is that I haven't been doing very well without you," she said. "I can't sleep at night, and when I do, my dreams are filled with you. I can't eat. I can't concentrate on my job…" She smiled awkwardly, sadly. "And I'm coming to learn that there are some facts I've got to face."

Claude simply looked at her, wondering if he'd ever seen anything so beautiful in his life.

"The first of which is that I love you."

His stomach clenched. She…loved…him.

Around him the bayou sang her song. Water trickled. Cypresses whispered. Birds fluttered.

Akela laughed without humor. "I know, that's probably the last thing you want to hear from any woman—"

Claude enfolded her in his arms so quickly she lost her balance. He immediately steadied her, burying his nose in her soft hair, breathing in her sweet, citrusy scent.

"Au contraire, chere," he murmured, holding her so tightly he was afraid he might be hurting her. "Those are exactly the words a hard, jaded man like me needed to hear." He pulled back to look at her, then kissed her lingeringly. "But not just from any woman. From you."

And right then, that moment, he vowed that while he might not be the man deserving of her love now, he would do all he could to be that man for the rest of their lives together.

Then he took her hand and led her to the house where Miss Daisy was setting the table for breakfast for three.

* * * * *

Look for the continuation of
Dangerous Liaisons with OBSESSION
in December 2005!

extreme Blaze

WHEN A STORY IS THIS DARING IT CAN ONLY BE CALLED EXTREME!

USA TODAY bestselling author

SUSAN KEARNEY

breaks through the boundaries of time
and sensuality as we know it in

Beyond the Edge

Wealthy businesswoman Fallon Hanover is sick of
being responsible. What she craves is some
excitement, adventure…and more important,
somebody else to be in control for a while.
Sexy stranger Kane Kincaid seems like
the perfect man to indulge herself with.
Until he tells her he's from the future….

On sale November 2005.

Available wherever books are sold.

If you enjoyed what you just read,
then we've got an offer you can't resist!

Take 2 bestselling
love stories FREE!

Plus get a FREE surprise gift!